NEW JUNGLE BOOK ADVENTURES

BEAR GRYLLS

RETURN TO THE JUNGLE

ILLUSTRATED BY
JAVIER JOAQUIN

MACMILLAN CHILDREN'S BOOKS

First published 2017 by Macmillan Children's Books
an imprint of Pan Macmillan
20 New Wharf Road, London N1 9RR
Associated companies throughout the world
www.panmacmillan.com

ISBN: 978-1-5098-5422-6

1 3 5 7 9 8 6 4 2

A CIP catalogue record for this book is available from the British Library.

Printed and bound by CPI Group (UK) Ltd, Croydon CR0 4YY

To my special youngest godchildren,
Rufus, Kitty, Caspar, Pip, Emily, Barney & Arlo

'We are the Pilgrims, master, we shall go always
a little further:
It may be beyond that last blue mountain barred
with snow,
Across that angry or that glimmering sea . . .'

Spiny R

River

Hills

Jungle

Mak &
Diya's
Route

Logging
Tow

CHAPTER ONE

India!

The word fluttered through Mak's head and made his pulse quicken. He was going back and he couldn't be happier.

He'd only been home for eight months, during which he'd ticked off a birthday and sat several exams, but the smell of the lush forests and the caress of the tropical breeze hadn't been forgotten. Even in smelly old London.

His previous trip would be considered a disaster by most people, especially his parents.

As they were travelling upriver to track big cats as part of a conservation project, a river swell had overturned their boat and separated him from his mother and father. For many days, he had been forced to march through the jungle to find his way back to them – foraging for food, navigating dangerous terrain and surviving encounters with lethal animals from leopards to hordes of bloodthirsty macaque monkeys.

It had been terrifying, brilliant and life changing!

While his parents might not agree with him, it had been the best learning experience a boy could have had. At first they had been overly protective of him, blaming themselves for what had happened. But little by little they'd noticed the change in Mak's attitude. Where he'd been shy, preferring to stay at home and avoid awkward social occasions, he now walked with a quiet confidence and seemed to have replaced fear with curiosity. So they allowed him to travel a little further, stay out a little longer.

His father would never admit it, but Mak could tell he was impressed by his son's new attitude. So, the moment his father had announced he must return to India for business, Mak had insisted that he go along.

As expected, his mother had been reluctant. She pointed out that Mak had shown he was confident enough to look after himself while they were away. Rather than argue, Mak had played along and told her he might throw a party at home while they were gone. That would get them to come round to his way of thinking!

He could see his parents' resolve slowly buckling. When he learned his father was going back to be honoured for his company's pioneering work in using technology for conservation, Mak had used the opportunity to tell him how proud he was and that the whole family should be there to watch. The plan worked, and his parents had eventually agreed with each other that Mak should come.

Mak packed his final items of clothing in the case sprawled across his bed – just a few shorts and T-shirts. In a small airtight bag he placed a few waterproof matches bought in Camden Market and a first-aid kit. This showed just how much he'd changed in the last few months. His previous love of video games had taken a back seat as he now consumed countless adventure books, eager to learn the most obscure and disgusting survival facts he could.

Mak still loved his magic, although it was no longer an escape for him – now it was more of a fun series of party tricks that everyone always seemed to love.

The final item to go into the case was an old penknife. It had been the first thing his father had given him when they'd returned to England. It had belonged to Mak's great-grandfather, who had served in the Second World War, and it had been passed down with many tales about how the knife had saved his life. Mak traced his finger along the notches in the wooden handle, and wondered what adventures his great-grandfather had been on. The blade was well oiled and as sharp as the day it had been forged.

Mak carefully placed it in a sock and closed the lid of his case.

'Makur!' came his mother's voice, summoning him downstairs.

This is it, he thought. *We're ready to go!*

He quickly zipped his case shut, snapped the locks in place and scrambled their combination codes. He tied up his sturdy hiking boots and raced downstairs, hauling the case as quickly as he could—

And slammed the corner of it into his sister's shin. Anula howled with pain.

'Mak, you idiot! Watch where you're going!'

Mak blinked in surprise. He thought Anula was still away at college, yet here she was, rubbing her shin and glaring at him with barely disguised anger.

'I'm going to have a massive bruise now!'

Their mother shook her head at him, but she knew better than to fuel an argument between the siblings.

'Anula, sorry. I didn't know you were back home.'

'Or what? You would have aimed for my head?' she snapped.

'I told you a dozen times, Makur,' his mother

said, 'but you've been in a world of your own ever since you knew we were going to India.'

Mak didn't recall any such conversation. He shrugged and turned to his sister. 'Are you house-sitting while we're away?' As he spoke, he noticed his father was moving three suitcases towards the front door.

Three more cases . . . His heart sank as the truth hit him.

'I wish,' snapped Anula. 'They're dragging me along . . . to keep an eye on you.'

If Anula didn't look pleased with the arrangement, then Mak's face showed that he felt even worse about it.

'Oh great.' The words caught in his throat. He coughed and forced a smile that made Anula's scowl deepen. 'But I don't need your help. I've shown that I can look after myself.' He poked her in the ribs. 'Maybe this time I'll be looking after *you*.'

He rolled his case to his father, ignoring the splutter of irritation from his sister.

CHAPTER TWO

'Little Wolf!'

Mak's head twisted as he tried to locate the speaker among the huge crowds at the arrival terminal. As the crowds receded, he saw a large card with the name 'MAKUR' scrawled on it in permanent marker. Underneath was the grinning face of Anil, the Indian who ran the conservation projects that his father's company used to field-test some of their technology. He had a wiry beard, and his dirt-stained clothes indicated that he'd just stepped out of the jungle.

Mak pushed closer and saw the grinning face of Anil's daughter, Diya, who was waving at him as she shouted again, 'Little Wolf!'

She wore a simple sari. He raised his hand to give her a fist-bump, but instead Diya yanked his forearm and pulled him closer. His breath was squeezed out of him in a crushing hug.

'It's so good to see you again, Little Wolf!' she exclaimed.

Mak gasped for breath as he pulled himself away and caught his sister looking quizzically at him.

'Little Wolf?' said Anula, rolling her eyes. 'Little Creep, more like.'

Mak met Diya's eyes and jerked his thumb towards his sister. 'This is my sister, Anula. Don't worry about her.'

Mak had assumed they were heading for the hotel, so was surprised when he was told their first port of call was Anil's latest conservation effort. They were heading straight for the jungle!

They rushed from the stale heat of the airport to a private heliport where they boarded a large helicopter to take them directly into the jungle, all paid for by the company his father had inherited from his uncle. While his parents were busily chatting with Anil, Mak was torn between gazing out of the large windows as the jungle rolled below them and chattering to Diya over the heavy headsets they wore to muffle the deep throb of the engine.

She had so much to tell him that it was a long time before he finally noticed his sister hadn't said a word. She looked pale as she stared at the jungle, her knuckles gripping her knees tightly. Mak couldn't resist a smile when she finally turned to him, her voice crackling over the intercom.

'You got lost in *that*?'

Mak nodded. 'Yeah, but in the really deep stuff. Not that little forest below.'

Anula's gaze turned back to the window and she shook her head. She'd heard the stories, but she'd never really asked Mak many questions about his adventure. He'd once overheard her comment that he'd probably made most of it up just to get sympathy.

Meanwhile, Mak had never seen the need to

argue with her, as he knew the truth. At least now he felt satisfied seeing the amazement on her face.

After two hours in the bone-shaking chopper, they landed in a small town, loaded their baggage into a pickup truck, and headed down a bumpy road through the fringes of the jungle.

Every so often huge lorries, laden with several wide logs strapped to their trailers, would thunder past in a cloud of dust and exhaust fumes. Other than that, there was no traffic.

'All this used to be jungle once,' said Diya sadly.

All Mak could see were rows of rectangular rice fields tended by farmers and the occasional ox pulling a plough.

From the driver's seat, her father addressed them, glancing at them now and again in the rearview mirror.

'At first the loggers moved in, cutting down everything in their path. Then the people followed, using the land to grow food. This road was once nothing more than a narrow track.'

'Isn't logging illegal?' Mak asked, gazing at the fields.

'Not all of it,' said Anil with a sigh. 'In this area it is all official, although it doesn't stop some of the more unscrupulous loggers from delving deeper into protected areas so they can reach rare hardwoods. But, legal or not, it scares the elephants away.'

Mak turned round sharply, and Diya smiled at the excitement in his eyes. 'I really want to see one. Are there elephants here?' he asked.

'Used to be,' said Anil. 'Asian elephants were very common in this area. Then people came and started capturing them to use as workers. Next came the loggers, destroying their habitat. We have over thirty thousand wild elephants in India, but here, in the central regions, no more than two and a half thousand, if we're lucky. And, with the logging, their numbers are decreasing.'

'Which is why we're out here,' said Mak's father with a smile. 'Our company has created a very special type of drone – and Anil is testing it for us.'

Anil nodded vigorously and glanced between Mak and Anula. 'You should be proud of your father. This project could revolutionize conservation as we know it!'

Mak had assumed they were returning to continue trials of the GPS tags that his father's company made. Anil had used them to track populations of big cats, and it had been one of these trackers that had eventually saved Mak's life. The idea of playing with drones was almost as exciting as meeting a real elephant.

After three hours of bouncing in the pickup, during which Anula had sat sulking with her earphones firmly in place, they reached the small logging town that Anil explained was going to be their base camp.

It looked just like any other small jungle town, with wooden shacks sporting rusting corrugated-iron roofs, electrical cables strung across the streets in gnarled clumps, and diesel-spewing trucks zipping across the street. Mak noticed a large group of tourists, laden down with cameras, filing into a local bar. Diya caught his gaze.

'The town is now attracting tourists who think they are "real" adventurers.' She giggled. 'Look at them, in their flip-flops, looking to "conquer" the jungle. All they do is walk a few metres to a waterfall –' she pointed to a muddy track as they passed – 'and then think they have seen it all.'

'That must be good for the local economy, bringing all that tourist money here,' Mak's father commented.

Anil shook his head. 'Sadly not. Their money attracts the wrong sort of people.' With a tilt of his head he indicated to their right-hand side as they passed a fenced-off area promising 'ELEPHANT RIDES'!

Mak craned his neck, trying to spot any elephants

beyond the fence, but instead only saw a sour-faced man, his pot belly hanging over his jeans, while his arms bulged with muscles under his shirt. The man's smile evaporated when he realized the pickup truck was not crammed with tourists.

Anil scowled. 'That's Buldeo. He caught a pair of elephants to use as entertainment, but took such poor care of them they died within months. Worked to death. He's a nasty piece of work, only interested in tourists brandishing a fistful of notes. With luck, he'll leave soon – especially now he knows we're here to keep an eye on him. My advice is for you to keep away from him.'

Mak twisted in his seat to watch Buldeo disappearing through a gate. As it swung closed, Mak swore he could see a large brown-grey *thing* in the paddock beyond, tufts of spiky hair poking from its head highlighted in the sun.

Then the gate closed, obscuring his view.

CHAPTER THREE

'There is no elephant,' said Mak for the third time, over the snort of teasing laughter from Diya.

'They're right in front of you!' she said.

Mak squinted at the thick forest displayed on the monitor, then looked back at her. 'This isn't getting lost in translation, is it? Does "elephant" in Hindi mean "tree" or something? We are talking about the same animal? Big, flappy ears, large trunk?'

Diya pouted and nudged him aside. She tapped the monitor. 'Right there. There are three of them.'

Mak glanced at the greasy smudge her finger had left on the screen and was about reply when he saw something move. At first he thought it was just the leaves blowing in the wind, but gradually he realized it was something huge moving behind the trees. A fully grown elephant.

Like an optical illusion, the moment he saw one, the other two became obvious, walking in single file along a narrow track.

'Wow!' Mak murmured. He was surprised to hear his sister draw a sharp intake of breath when she finally saw them too. His whole family was crowded around the large screen watching footage from the drone. Anil was piloting it with a joystick and a computer keyboard, but the drone itself was many miles from them, hovering high over the jungle canopy. Its powerful cameras were trained on the ground and beaming live images back to base camp.

'That's the herd we've been tracking,' said Anil proudly. 'As soon as I heard about the fight to save the elephants out here, I volunteered our services – all thanks to your father.'

A proud smile flickered across his father's face. 'It's a new type of drone. More like an airship than an aeroplane. It's able to hover over the same area for weeks, and can even automatically track and follow herds at walking pace. The high-definition camera offers unparalleled detail – and it's all broadcasted back here, complete with GPS data.'

As he spoke, Anil zoomed the camera in so closely they could see the elephant's long eyelashes, the patchwork of wrinkled pink-and-brown skin.

'She's the leader,' commented Anil. 'There are thirteen of them in the herd.'

'Where are her tusks?' said Mak.

'All African elephants have them,' said Diya in her best teacher's voice, 'but generally not the female Indian elephant. And, if they do, we call them *tushes*, not tusks.'

'I can't believe something so big is so difficult to see,' said Anula, finally unable to hide her interest.

Anil smiled. 'They're perfectly camouflaged for their environment. There could be one just a few metres in front of you, and you wouldn't see or hear it in the jungle. They can tread almost silently, and with their trunks they can pick up an insect off the ground. Cool, eh? They are like the ninjas of the jungle.'

'That's difficult to believe,' said Mak, his eyes glued to the screen as the drone slowly circled so that more members of the herd became visible. Mak watched Anil skilfully nudge the joystick, and the drone responded almost immediately. It was like a real-life video game.

Anil sniffed. 'That is also why they're so difficult to track. They're too big to tranquillize and put radio collars on to them, like we do with the big cats. And now they're heading into the deepest jungle to distance themselves from the loggers. This herd has been on the move for a week since loggers began scaring them.'

Diya leaned closer to the screen. Her smile had transformed into a deep frown.

'I can't see Hathi.'

Anil zoomed the camera out so they could now see all the herd moving like phantoms through the trees. Both he and Diya counted under their breath.

'There are only twelve of them! He's missing!' Diya exclaimed.

Anil shook his head. 'No. He must be there somewhere.'

Mak exchanged a confused look with Diya. 'Who's missing?'

'Hathi! He's a calf. The newest member of the herd. We think he's only about ten months old. He always stays close to his mother. He wouldn't have wandered off.'

Anil panned the camera around, but there was no sight of the young elephant. He glanced at a computer screen, which showed the drone's position on a map. A wriggling line represented the movement of the aircraft since it had been tracking the elephants, and there was no mistaking a sharp U-turn in the herd's path.

'They've turned round!' Anil exclaimed.

Diya zoomed out of the map until they could see their own location twenty kilometres away. The herd had plainly been walking away until they'd recently turned back on themselves. Diya traced a finger in a straight line from the herd's trajectory. It headed straight back to the logging town.

'Why would they be coming here?' asked Mak.

'They're not,' said Anil, but there was doubt in his voice. 'It looks as if they've turned to search for Hathi.'

Mak's mother spoke up. 'Is that common behaviour?'

Anil hesitated before answering. 'They are very protective of their children. Just as we are.' His eyes shot to Mak as if to emphasize his point. 'But I have never witnessed this before . . .'

Mak pointed to a network of black lines running through the jungle. The elephants had crossed over a couple of them. 'Are those roads?'

'Trails made by the loggers,' Anil growled. 'They cut down anything in their way to get deeper inside.' He pointed to a spec on the map that lay near a distinctive V-shaped valley. 'The roads were originally used by farmers here. They use the flanks of these limestone hills to grow fruit and rice; they're harsh slopes that they call Spiny Ridge, but the land is fertile. The farmers are no friends of the elephants, though,' he added darkly. 'To them, the elephants are a threat to their crops and land.'

'Do you think the herd knows where Hathi is?'

asked Anula, engrossed in the drama.

Anil sighed. 'It's so sad to lose one so young, but sometimes it is nature's way. He could have had an accident, been attacked . . . Who knows? Unfortunately, it happens. It can't be helped. That is the law of the jungle, after all.'

'But surely if that had happened, the rest of the herd would know and wouldn't be looking for him now?' said Mak.

Anil shook his head. He didn't know. Yet somehow Mak had a horrible feeling *he* knew. He gripped Diya's arm and gently pulled her to the hut door where he spoke softly to her.

'This might sound crazy –' he checked the others were not listening – 'but do you think Hathi may have been elephant-napped?'

CHAPTER FOUR

The sad news of Hathi's loss cast a sombre atmosphere over the camp. Darkness fell and they settled down for supper. Mak's family were all yawning before the meal of rice, chicken curry and coconut had finished. Jet lag was catching up with them.

Mak, on the other hand, was feeling energized. It was as if an electric charge was coursing through him, unleashed just as the trees around them came alive with frogs, bats and insects in their nightly chorus. The air smelt sharp, damp and fresh – completely unlike the stale streets of London. And with it came clear memories of sleeping with wild wolves and running through the boughs of mighty trees.

He felt *alive* here!

Hathi's disappearance weighed heavily on Diya's shoulders, and she had said little all evening. She hadn't questioned Mak's fears about Hathi, and they'd both agreed to talk later.

Mak's parents settled down to bed, while Anula made constant whimpering noises from her cabin every time she heard an insect scampering through her room. As for Anil, he was back inside the building containing the drone controls, poring over the data.

Mak and Diya sneaked to the edge of the camp, desperate not to draw attention to themselves. The slightest thing would set off Mak's parents worrying.

'Buldeo doesn't have elephants any more,' Diya said in a whisper that was almost as loud as her normal voice.

Mak waved his hands to indicate she needed to be quieter. 'All I can tell you is what I saw when we drove past this afternoon. There was something inside. At first I thought it was a horse.'

'Horses and elephants look very different!'

'I know that!' Mak sighed. 'It was only a quick glimpse before the gate shut. And it looked a little hairy, so I thought of a horse . . .'

'Young elephants have a lot of downy hairs,' Diya said thoughtfully, 'but they still don't look like horses.' Mak could see that she was starting to feel curious. 'And it sounds like a coincidence,' she added, as if to convince herself.

'All I'm saying is I think it's worth checking it out. You said he's taken elephants before. What's stopping him from doing it again?' He could see she was torn. 'You saw the dirt roads on the monitor. What if Hathi stumbled down one and has been taken by a bunch of passing loggers?'

Diya sighed. 'OK. Let's go and investigate. But we can't do anything stupid.'

'Cross my heart,' Mak said, licking his finger and crossing his chest.

Diya led the way across the camp.

Mak noticed that she'd changed from her sari to a pair of sensible jungle trousers and shirt. He couldn't help but think that Diya hadn't needed persuading. The scent of the jungle had rekindled a thirst for adventure in Mak.

And now he was determined to have one.

It wasn't exactly difficult to break into Buldeo's paddock. Aside from some barbed wire along the top of the fence, placed there more to keep mischievous monkeys out than people, there was no security. The main gate was locked from the inside by a wooden bar drawn across the middle – not that it mattered, as the wood on the bottom of the gate had rotted away so Mak and Diya could easily scramble underneath, flat on their stomachs.

Inside, Mak and Diya crawled for cover behind a wooden trough. The smell of fetid water coming from it made them gag. A pair of floodlights attracted swarms of moths and cast a faint light on a sorry-looking circle of dried grass and mud.

A heap of mouldy hay lay to one side. They crawled over and peered round it. At the edge of the circle of dried grass, they then saw it. A miserable young elephant stood in the shadows, head down and gently swaying. The animal was hardly as tall as Mak.

Mak and Diya could see that the poor elephant was tightly shackled round one leg by a rusty chain, the other end of which was fastened to a stake in the ground.

A sudden noise made them jump.

The gate swung open and the pair watched as Buldeo strode purposefully into the compound.

They both ducked down low behind the trough and held their breath.

Buldeo then approached the elephant with two muscular Indian men. One was drinking a beer from a bottle, while the other held a long pole, tipped with a spike and a cruel-looking hook-shaped blade. He poked the baby elephant with it, causing it to give a squeaky bellow and raise its trunk defiantly.

'Stupid animal!' the man muttered. 'You have to learn who your *mahout* is!'

'Easy, Girish,' said Buldeo, pushing the man's weapon down. 'We don't want to damage the merchandise. Nobody wants pictures of their children riding a half-dead elephant. And, remember, if this doesn't work out then I'm broke! And if I'm broke, then you two won't get paid and we'll all be on the streets!'

'You want it trained or not?' huffed Girish.

From behind the trough, Mak and Diya watched as Girish poked the elephant again.

'That's definitely Hathi,' said Diya through gritted teeth. 'And if he pokes that *goad* into him again, I swear I'll . . .' She took a deep breath to calm herself. 'We have to go back and tell my father.'

'But we can't leave Hathi like this,' said Mak as Buldeo yanked on the chain, causing Hathi to stumble. The man yelled abuse at the elephant for not following instructions. 'And, anyway, all your dad will do is go and notify the police, and it doesn't look like there are many out here. It could take days for them to arrive.'

'Then what do you suggest?' Even in the shadows, Diya could see the gleam in Mak's eyes.

'I suggest we wait . . . then we spring him loose!'

CHAPTER FIVE

As much as they hated to sit and watch Buldeo, Girish and Lalu, the drunk bully, shove and poke Hathi, there was nothing they could do to stop them.

Using the cruel *goad*, they were attempting to train the elephant to raise his foreleg and salute his trunk on Buldeo's command, something the men no doubt thought would encourage tourists to part with their money.

It was close to ten o'clock before the thugs gave up and left the compound. The lights were extinguished, leaving Hathi standing on his own in the darkness, mewing pitifully.

As soon as they heard the receding *put-put* of the men's scooters beyond the gate, Mak and Diya emerged from the shadows, shining their torches to illuminate both the elephant and themselves so that Hathi wouldn't be too alarmed.

Mak was surprised that the elephant didn't react

badly. Instead Hathi regarded them from behind his long eyelashes, allowing them to get close.

'Don't be afraid,' cooed Mak in a soothing voice.

'He's not,' Diya said. 'Elephants have an amazing sense of smell. They can even sniff out water. And they're smart too. He knew we were here from the moment we arrived.'

Mak followed the end of the chain to the spike in the ground and tugged at it. 'Smarter than those idiots, that's for sure.' The spike wouldn't budge. He turned to see Diya and Hathi watching him.

'Smarter than you, it seems,' Diya said teasingly as she began to loosen the chain round Hathi's knee, instead of wrestling with the large spike in the ground.

The loosened chain dropped away from Hathi's leg and clattered to the floor. The elephant pulled its leg free but didn't move, eyeing the children with caution. Diya waved Mak over.

'Come and say hello.'

Mak warily drew closer. Hathi stood almost as tall as he did. Fine hairs covered his body. Ears gently flapped to cool himself in the humid night, while a slender tail twitched to keep flies at bay. Mak stopped in his tracks when he was close enough for the elephant to raise his trunk and snuffle it across his chest. He couldn't stop chuckling as the trunk brushed over his face.

'It's like being kissed by a vacuum cleaner!'

He tentatively reached out a hand and gently ran it across the soft bristles on Hathi's head. The elephant responded with a cute warble. Mak couldn't believe he was actually touching an elephant.

'I think he likes us,' said Diya as the trunk rummaged through her hair. 'So, we have an elephant. Now what?'

Mak shone his torch around the stark compound. 'We get him out of here.'

'He could come back to our camp.'

'He could,' Mak said slowly, 'but it wouldn't take long for word to reach Buldeo. Then what? Your father's organization would have to fight those idiots just to keep Hathi safe.'

A different plan was already forming in his head. It was daring, risky and he had no idea how Diya would react to it.

She shone her torch directly into his face, forcing him to shield his eyes and look away. 'I know that look,' she said. 'You promised me nothing stupid – and we have already broken into private property and unchained an elephant!'

'It's not stupid, honestly!'

'Then what are you thinking?'

'What if we took him straight to his home?'

Since arriving back in India, he was feeling an ever-growing desire to return to the jungle. The very thought of it filled his stomach with butterflies. Now he had a proper excuse to do so.

Diya had temporarily ruined his night vision when she'd shone the torch into his eyes, so he couldn't see her reaction. But he could hear her voice.

'Our parents would go crazy!'

'We could keep in touch using a satellite phone, and Anula could cover for us.'

'I doubt your sister would want to do anything to help you.'

'She's not that bad,' replied Mak. 'Anyway, if she lets on that we're missing, then my parents will be just as mad at her as they would at me. She's supposed to be keeping an eye on me.' He gestured around. 'And the first night she's already done a terrible job. She's more worried about getting bugs in her hair!' He paused. 'Anyway, we won't be gone long, and what choice do we really have? We can't leave Hathi here like this.'

Now that his night vision was returning, he could see Diya was thoughtfully stroking Hathi's trunk, and the little elephant was responding by coiling it gently round her arm.

'I've been spending a few days in a nearby bird

hide, a kilometre into the jungle, cataloguing species for my father. He even allows me to sleep there sometimes . . .'

Mak was struck by a sudden doubt. 'Although if my dad did find out, this might be the last time I ever get to come back here. I wouldn't see the jungle again. Or you,' he added, blushing as he did so.

But Diya wasn't listening; she was forming her own plan.

'So, if we pretend to have gone off birdwatching, then we could get away with it.' She looked at him with a flash of excitement. 'I bet we'll only need a day to get Hathi to the herd. Maybe we tell your sister we're going and will be back by the end of the day.' She paused. 'Then if we're any longer, we'll just say we got a bit lost!'

Mak smiled slowly. 'That sounds like a plan,' he said. 'But the first thing we have to do is get Hathi out of here!'

CHAPTER SIX

The splintering wood sounded unnaturally loud in the quiet street. The wooden hinges split with a piercing crack, and then hung limp, swinging gently on the remaining strands of wood that held them in place. Mak held his breath waiting for somebody to run out and yell at them, but was greeted by silence.

They'd found the paddock gate secured from the outside by a thick chain and rusty padlock. When it showed no sign of giving way, Mak started looking for another escape route, but he didn't need to bother.

Mak had hardly turned his back when Hathi had simply pushed hard up against the gate and they'd burst outward like the floodgates of a dam being breached.

'Well, we're out!' exclaimed Diya as they looked around the empty street. 'Now what?'

Hathi stood there swinging his trunk with a look

of wild excitement in his eyes. It was the first sign of the playful nature that Diya knew young elephants should have – and it had helped them too!

But Mak was already planning the next steps in his head. 'First, we need to go back to camp for a few supplies.'

'That means cutting across town,' Diya warned.

'But will she follow us?' Mak asked.

'Let's find out.'

They didn't need to worry. As soon as they moved out of the paddock, Hathi started to follow them.

'Good boy, Hathi. Keep coming now!' Mak praised as they walked.

There were no street lamps, but they still kept to the edge of the road, avoiding the occasional pools of light cast out by the buildings they passed.

Mak and Diya noticed almost at once that they were both making much more noise walking down the street than the elephant did. Their boots scuffed on the tarmac and they kept kicking bottles and plastic rubbish that they didn't spot in the dark. Meanwhile Hathi's steps were strangely silent.

The roadside was filled with litter – discarded cans, bottles, rolls of wire mesh and bits of corrugated iron destined for buildings that were never made. Yet Hathi negotiated them all silently.

Suddenly they saw bright lights about two hundred metres ahead. The loud chatter of raised voices and thumping Hindi pop music made them stop in their tracks.

'It's the local bar,' Diya warned as they stopped in the shadows and stared down the street.

The road ahead was thick with parked scooters. It seemed that every truck driver and logger in the town was crammed inside. People spilled out of the doorway clutching beer bottles and attempting to cool down from the sickly hot interior.

'The track is about fifty metres past that bar.' Diya pointed ahead. 'There's no way we can smuggle an elephant past them!'

As they stood there trying to think what to do, Mak suddenly grabbed Diya.

'Look – there's Buldeo!'

Sure enough, Buldeo and his two henchmen were standing on the porch, holding drinks and talking animatedly to a group of mean-looking loggers.

Diya sighed in defeat, but Mak was already looking around for a solution.

'I've got an idea!'

If Mak's hobby as a magician had taught him anything, it was that the best distractions always worked when they were in plain sight.

So when Lalu happened to glance in their

direction, all he saw were two kids carrying a large sheet of plywood between them. Just a couple of street kids carrying whatever they could to make a shelter for the night.

It was only when he noticed four big feet under the wood that Lalu peered drunkenly at his bottle, wondering if he'd had enough. When he looked back into the street, the kids and their walking plank had disappeared into the darkness.

CHAPTER SEVEN

Anula lay in her bed with the thin sheet tucked tightly to her chin to prevent any insects from joining her in the night. Although she was exhausted with jet lag, the oppressive heat and constant strange chirping from the darkness outside was keeping her wide awake.

She'd found an internet connection in base camp, and had spent most of the evening listening to music and looking up what all her friends were doing on Facebook.

'Go away, Mak,' she said from under the sheets.

'I'm just seeing if you're busy.'

'Oh yeah, sure. I mean, there's soooo much to do here.' Her voice was laden with sarcasm. 'Go to sleep, Makur. It's the middle of the night. Babysitting you is the worst.'

Mak bit back his natural instinct to argue the word 'babysitting', and instead put forward his idea.

'Diya and I can't sleep, so we're going bird-watching to see the sunrise. There's a hide that Diya's dad knows about that's meant to be amazing. You want to come and join us for a sleep there?' He paused. 'With all the animals all around.'

That bit will put her off for sure, he thought, smiling to himself.

Anula sat up in bed. 'You want me to come and sleep over with you and your little friend, in a hut, in the jungle?'

For a dreadful moment Mak thought she was going to agree. Then he saw the horrified expression creeping across her face.

'I couldn't think of anything worse,' she sneered. 'You both do whatever you want. Just don't get me into trouble and make sure you're back by breakfast.'

Mak pretended to be disappointed. 'Oh, OK, then. And we will, I promise.' He paused. 'We'll take the sat phone just in case, so you can always check in with me if you want to talk.'

'Like I want to do that.' And she lay back down.

Mak quietly left his sister's hut, feeling confident she'd fallen for the story. He darted to his own room and quickly packed, shoving the survival gear he'd brought from England into his satchel, and remembering his pocketknife.

He also scribbled a quick note, which he left

on his bed, saying that he and Diya had gone birdwatching and would be back at the end of the day. By leaving the note and talking to Anula about their 'birdwatching' plan, he figured they should be covered, at least for the rest of the night and the following day.

Mak had left Diya at the tourist waterfall just on the edge of town, stroking Hathi's nose and trying to keep the elephant calm.

She kept looking at her watch, willing Mak to hurry up. They needed to get moving.

Mak left his bedroom and then sneaked into the drone command building, which was now dark since Anil had powered down the monitors and left for bed.

Following Diya's instructions, he found a satellite phone, an old cooking pan that had been used to capture drips during a storm, a small printed map of the area, two spare torches, several energy bars stashed in a box under the desk, and a water-purification flask, which he filled to the brim. Grabbing a small backpack in which to carry the extra equipment, Mak crept out of the building.

On his way out of the camp, he retrieved a machete that had been thrust into a firewood pile.

He carefully slid it into its sheath and fastened it to his belt.

Then he dashed off to meet Diya and Hathi where he'd left them.

So far, all was going to plan.

CHAPTER EIGHT

Mak's joyful whoops echoed from the rock face as he punched the air. Any fear of them being overheard was drowned out by a waterfall.

'We're on our way!' cried Mak.

Mak took in the waterfall and the forest around them. It was a tiny cascade compared to those he'd seen before, but the smell of running water and the wet forest cast aside any fatigue he'd been feeling. Hathi was already knee-deep in the water, enjoying the fresh taste and squirting it over himself with delight.

Mak glanced at the luminous dials on his wristwatch. It wasn't even eleven o'clock yet.

'We need to push on – as far as we can, as fast as we can – to reach the herd,' he said.

He handed Diya the backpack of supplies and took a paper map and a marker pen from his satchel. He unfolded the map and circled the logging town,

then traced his finger north-west across the jungle to where he'd memorized the herd's location.

'The herd is moving in this direction. Hopefully we can head straight through the jungle and intercept them here.' He tapped the distinctive V-shaped valley that marked the end of Spiny Ridge. He recalled that the farming village Anil had shown them wasn't very far away, but it wasn't marked on the map. Neither were the logging tracks. Instead, there was just a spaghetti knot of streams and waterways that fed into a sinuous single river leading off the map.

He directed his torch beam to a narrow trail that led into the jungle at the foot of the waterfall. Even in the waning moonlight, they could see that it went gently upwards as it entered the forest.

'That's the way we need to be going if we're going to reach the herd.'

Diya smiled. 'Let's do this, jungle boy!'

She then took a moment to split their equipment more evenly between her backpack and his satchel, while Mak laid a hand on the side of the elephant's head and scratched gently.

'Well, Hathi, we're going to get you back to your mum, but you're going to have to help us – and trust us.'

Hathi responded by coiling his trunk round Mak's arm and giving him a gentle fan with his broad ears. Mak hoped that was the elephant equivalent of 'OK'.

He cocked his head, seeing that Diya was looking really concerned.

'You really think they'll come all the way out here to search for Hathi?' Diya said.

Mak swept his torch beam across the dirt floor. Hathi's heavy footprints could be seen clearly in the earth.

'Elephants are not quite as difficult to miss as your dad made out.'

He could see the fear written on Diya's face. Mak moved closer and laid a hand on her shoulder. 'It's going to be fine. We can do this. Together.' He paused. 'But we need to keep moving as far as we can. After all, somebody is relying on us.'

They both looked at Hathi, who was still frolicking in the water, revelling in his newfound freedom. The sight of the animal cast some of the doubt from Diya's mind. She nodded firmly.

'Let's go, then.' She marched towards the trail.

'Are you coming or what?' Mak said, whistling to Hathi and turning to follow Diya.

The elephant trotted from the pool and caught up with Mak. It was as if Hathi sensed what their plan was and was eager to find his way home.

For the next few hours they tramped along the trail, pushing undergrowth aside. The moonlight occasionally helped illuminate the path ahead, and Mak instructed Diya to turn their torches off to save the battery life. In his haste to leave, he hadn't thought to bring spares.

One thing Mak was grateful for bringing was the machete. For the first hour the trail was manageable, but as the foliage around them grew, blocking the faint moonlight and allowing the hoots and chitters of jungle life to rise in volume, the path became more difficult.

Mak swung the machete to hack at the branches and vines criss-crossing their path, but more often than not the blade would rebound on the tougher plants.

He felt Diya grip his shoulder to stop him. 'Stop waving your arms like a windmill!' She prised the machete from his grip. 'If you keep doing it that way, you'll chop off one of your limbs! You need to make short but firm strokes, like this.'

Mak watched as Diya kept her free arm close to her body, wielding the blade in strong, controlled movements, slashing through the vines and branches with ease. He and Hathi followed on behind as she cut her way effortlessly through the undergrowth.

'I get it now,' Mak said. 'I can do this.' He paused. 'Thanks for the advice though.'

'No worries. We're a team, as you said.'

Mak continued cutting his way through out front, working hard. The pair soon lost track of time, but they were making quick progress now along the trail into the thick jungle.

Eventually Mak thrust the point of the machete

into the side of a big tree and leaned on it to catch his breath.

'My arm is going to fall off!' He sighed.

'My time to take over, then,' Diya replied, with no hesitation.

'Roger that!'

Mak smiled. *This girl is tough*, he thought.

And with that, the pair pressed on.

An hour later though, both Mak and Diya were dead beat. The adrenaline, heat and physically demanding work of jungle travel was taking its toll on both of them.

Mak called a halt and shone his torch around a small natural clearing they'd come to. The ground was thick with bushes and tangles of branches that rose around the mighty curving roots of a huge tree – the perfect place to sleep.

'I think we've found our camp,' he said.

CHAPTER NINE

Anula woke after far too little sleep. Her blankets had been pulled so tight to combat intrusive insects that she could barely move. Her mother was at her door, glancing around the room with concern.

'Have you seen Makur?' she asked, her voice full of worry.

'Oh, yeah . . .' Anula murmured groggily. She just wanted to roll over and go back to sleep. 'He told me he's gone birdwatching . . . Diya has a hut or something. Her dad knows.'

'Anil knows?'

Anula could barely find the energy to speak. 'Sure. She goes there all the time apparently. Sleeps over. Counts birds.'

'Well, I do remember Anil mentioning something about that. They must have left early.'

'Yeah . . . I've barely slept, Mum.'

Her mother relaxed, assured that Anula had seen

them earlier. 'Thank goodness for that. After last time, your father and I have been so concerned . . . That's exactly why we wanted you here.'

'I'm on top of it,' said Anula sleepily as she rolled over and yawned. 'And I told him to take the satellite phone. So relax. I'll let you know if there are any problems . . .'

Then she was asleep. Her mother left quietly, cross with Mak for not asking first, but happy that there was nothing to worry about.

Mak woke with his nose itching. He squinted through a ray of light peeking between the boughs above and focused on a butterfly perched on his nose. It was huge and he could clearly see its proboscis drinking the sweat trickling down his face.

When he gave a gentle sniff, the butterfly fluttered away. He sat up to see Diya was asleep in a tight ball, with a waterproof sheet that she'd had in her pack wrapped tightly round her. Mak stretched and joined Hathi, who was snuffling around the foliage, his nimble trunk picking at fine green shoots and stems of bamboo just as fast as he could.

'You're hungry, huh?' Mak said, his own stomach rumbling on cue. He'd packed several energy bars in his satchel and some vacuum-packed rice, but he wanted to save those in case of any emergency, so he too picked some of the succulent bamboo growing around him and chewed on it.

'What are you doing?' Diya asked as she woke up to see Mak racing against the elephant to eat the bamboo shoots.

'Morning! Want some bamboo?' He tossed a stem to Diya, who ate it before taking an energy bar from her own pack.

'Much more filling!' she said, taking a bite. She looked around, completely disorientated. 'Which way do we go?'

Mak filled his mouth with more bamboo, then opened his pack and rooted through it. There was something missing. 'Do you have the map?'

'The map? No. You were carrying it,' Diya said with alarm.

Mak searched the area around his pack, just in case it had fallen out. 'It's not here.' He saw the look of panic on Diya's face.

'It must be here.'

The pair frantically searched through all their gear and pockets. But nothing.

They slumped down silently and then stared at each other.

This was bad.

'Maybe we don't actually need it,' Mak commented, trying to put a positive spin on it.

'*We don't need it?*' Diya repeated in surprise. 'I don't want to get lost out here!'

'No chance,' Mak said confidently. He helped her stand and checked his watch before locating the position of the sun through the trees. 'Look, it's not quite seven o'clock yet, and the sun is over there.'

'And how does that help us?'

Mak took his watch off and slowly turned it in his hand so that the hour hand was pointing at the sun. Then he gestured in the direction halfway between twelve o'clock and the hour hand.

'That is south. Which means north-west is –' he circled round and pointed – 'that way. The herd has been moving steadily from that direction, so we should be able to intercept them.'

He picked up his pack and whistled to Hathi. The elephant immediately responded and trotted in pursuit. Diya shook her head and hid her smile. She was impressed. Although she didn't want Mak to see that.

Buldeo's screams of rage echoed through the compound. He kicked at the chain on the floor, but that did nothing more than painfully stub his toe.

'You didn't tighten the chain enough!' he bellowed, waving a finger at Girish. 'It's your fault!'

Girish rubbed his temple. He'd woken up with a

headache and the last thing he needed was his boss shouting at him. He knelt down to inspect the chain.

'There's nothing wrong with this chain,' he said, running it through his fingers. 'Somebody took it off the animal.'

Lalu struggled to lift up one of the broken gates that had fallen into the road. He grunted with the effort of propping it up against the side of the building.

'And then it must have burst through this,' Lalu said.

Buldeo wasn't listening. Something had caught his eye, and he crouched in the dirt. The elephant's footprints circled round and led straight towards the gate, confirming Lalu's theory.

Lalu crouched in the road and traced his fingers around several dirt marks.

'He went this way.' He indicated down the street.

Buldeo and Girish exchanged an uncertain look.

'Are you sure?' Buldeo asked. 'That looks like some mud splatters from a truck.'

Lalu shook his head. 'I'm the tracker. I know what an elephant's print looks like. And he went this way.'

Lalu set off down the road, Buldeo and Girish following quickly behind. Buldeo would march all day if necessary to get his prize back.

His future and the future of the two goons he employed were at stake.

He wouldn't let anything, or anybody, get in his way . . .

CHAPTER TEN

The morning was glorious, and Mak couldn't remember seeing the jungle more alive, even when he'd been living in it for weeks. Flowers were in bloom, insects flitting from one to the other. Butterflies danced, fat bees bobbed lazily through the air, and birds sang from every tree.

The forest provided a much easier walk now, with many clearings and wide tracks for them to venture through. There was no need to break out the machete again as the trees thinned to make way for the waist-high grass and red and yellow flowers that lay before them.

Mak had learned that where loggers had previously cleared the jungle, the undergrowth grew back thick and ugly, as the sunlight could now reach down to the jungle floor. This was called secondary jungle, and it was horrible to hike through. As Mak and Diya had discovered the day before.

But now they were in primary jungle, where the trees grew straight and tall, and the ground itself was much clearer and less cluttered than the dense thorny undergrowth of the earlier part of their journey.

Soon the trio popped out into a larger clearing. As they meandered through the knee-high grass of the meadow, it came alive with swarms of colourful butterflies that scattered to avoid them. Hathi enjoyed swatting his trunk to catch them, but behaved himself and kept close to Diya.

Pausing to pick some head-sized spiky jack fruit from the tree, which Diya expertly carved into eatable portions with the machete, Mak's mind began to wander.

Every step he made took him back to the time he'd been lost in the jungle. He remembered that it had been such a frightening, lonely experience. If it hadn't been for the wolves who'd adopted him, then he had no doubt he would have died out there. Even so, his memories of the experience were amazing, and he couldn't help comparing it to living in the grey concrete slabs of London where his family lived.

He was vaguely aware that Diya was talking to him, but his mind was fantasizing about building a cabin and living in the wild. Even the bizarreness of guiding a young elephant calf home through the dense jungle felt normal, exciting . . .

'Little Wolf?' Diya's voice was raised. She'd obviously been calling him a few times. 'Oh, you're back with us. That's nice. Hello.' She gestured ahead of them.

A wide river cut along their path. The water was brown and slow moving. A few floating tree branches further out hinted that it was deep. They stood on an elevated bank that sloped down a couple of metres to the sandy shore below. A shore that was being patrolled by a pair of large grey herons, their javelin beaks poised above the water, waiting for their prey to swim past.

Mak caught the uncertain look on Diya's face. 'Relax. This was on the map. This is useful, in fact. It curves westward that way.' He indicated upstream. 'If we follow the shore, then we can stay out of the denser jungle and increase our speed.'

Diya looked suspiciously at him. 'Are you sure you know where we're going?'

Mak patted Hathi's flank. The little elephant had stopped with them and made no attempt to head to the water's edge. 'Trust me, I want to see Hathi reunited with his mum just as must as you do.'

Diya still wasn't convinced. 'It's just that . . .' She looked away, suddenly embarrassed.

'What?'

She sighed and gestured around. 'I have seen the look on your face now we're here. It is like you are lost in your own world. I worry that you want to stay here forever.'

'Don't *you*? I mean . . . look around!' Mak hopped down the bank to the shore, causing the herons to take flight. One swooped across the river, landing on a floating log to resume fishing. 'It's special out here. So peaceful. So full of life.' He caught the look on her face. 'Don't worry. I'm not going to get us lost. We'll sort Hathi out, then get back to the camp. But after that . . . well . . . what if I stayed?'

'In India?'

Mak had meant the jungle. He knew his parents wouldn't let him, but his mind jumped to the idea of running away.

He shrugged. 'Sure. India,' he said. 'I could stay with you and your dad . . .'

'Little Wolf . . .'

'Help with conservation work.' Even as he said it, it sounded a wonderful idea.

'Mak!'

Mak's excitement was growing and he began pacing. 'I could even work for my dad's company over here!'

'Don't move!' Diya hissed.

Mak stopped in his tracks in time to hear the undergrowth close by shudder as something large moved through it. His hand went for the machete on his belt.

It wasn't there.

He looked up to see Diya had it in her hand. Behind her, Hathi stood motionless, his ears fanning out wide in an unmistakable threatening gesture.

Mak slowly turned to the undergrowth again as branches snapped. Something was coming his way . . .

CHAPTER ELEVEN

Just from the sound of the twigs snapping, Mak could tell something large was in the undergrowth – and he was standing on the open sandy shore, completely defenceless. He cursed himself for being so complacent. The smells and sights around him had brought nothing but good memories, but now he recalled the rabid monkeys, the lethal leopards and the other dangers that also call the jungle home.

And one of them was in the undergrowth right in front of him, no doubt looking for its next meal.

Mak spotted a sturdy-looking tree branch lying in the sand just a metre away. It had broken at an angle, creating a natural sharp spear tip. The only problem was that he'd have to run towards the unseen monster to reach it.

Without thinking, Mak suddenly charged forward, yelling at the top of his lungs. He snatched the stick up and hefted it over his shoulder, ready to stab anything hungry enough to have a go at him.

There was an explosion of movement in the foliage. Whatever was there moved with a sudden spurt of speed, kicking up loose plants and wet sand as it moved. But it wasn't heading for Mak – it was running away.

They all heard a gentle splash as whatever had been stalking him vanished into a small lagoon that lay just behind the undergrowth, separated from the river by a few metres.

Mak's heart was pounding and his ears throbbed from the blood pumping in them. He felt light-headed and giddy as adrenaline coursed through him. Then he realized Diya was clapping.

'That was very brave!' Diya said as she ran down the embankment to his side. Hathi followed more cautiously. 'And one heck of a battle cry!'

It took Mak a few more seconds to calm down and realize what he'd instinctively done. Fight or flight, mankind's oldest instinct. In the past, Mak had always chosen flight, to run from whatever dangers threatened him. But something had changed and he'd found a reservoir of courage he hadn't known he possessed.

Maybe fear had caused him to act so rashly? Or perhaps he'd wanted to protect Diya and Hathi? Either way, it had worked.

'You scared it off with your screaming!' Diya laughed.

The burst of adrenaline, released by his body to sharpen Mak's reactions and senses, was wearing off, and he felt a little sick.

'That was the plan,' he said weakly, lowering his new spear so she couldn't see that his hand was now trembling. 'I wonder what it was?'

He drew closer to the undergrowth, the spear aimed forward. He poked around, but nothing stirred. Standing on tiptoes, he could see across the lagoon beyond. There was no sign of movement there.

'Could have been a wild boar?' Mak suggested. 'Or a jungle cat?' There were plenty of other feline predators alongside the more famous leopards, and they were powerful swimmers, a technique that helped them catch prey unaware.

Diya shook her head. 'It was bigger than that. And if it was a big cat, it would have attacked.' She began inspecting the sand at the edge of the river, her voice dropping with concern. 'The loggers used to tell my father stories about things they saw out here.'

'What kind of things?'

Diya hesitated, unsure whether she should continue.

Mak pressed her. 'You can't say that and then keep me in suspense.'

'Loggers are often the very first people to enter remote habitats. They claim to have seen tigers where there are supposed to be none.'

The mention of a tiger sent both a thrill and chill through Mak. He'd only seen a tiger in a zoo back home, and the poor thing had looked so miserable in its cage. He longed to see a wild one – but perhaps not this up close and personal.

Diya didn't see his worried look and continued in a low voice as she searched the shoreline. 'One mining expedition lost a man. Said he'd been eaten by an enormous python.'

Mak had seen pythons before, but none had looked big enough to eat a person – especially not the men who often joined mining teams. For one of those miners to have been eaten, the monster would have to be the length of a lorry . . .

'And then there are also the crocodiles.' The tone of her voice made Mak look up. Diya was pointing to a set of huge crocodilian footprints. She placed her hand on one and splayed her fingers as wide as she could. The footprint was still larger. These tracks, along with the distinctive furrow created by its heavy tail, led towards the river, indicating that it wasn't what had been in the bush.

'Big ones have been known to attack people. Even baby elephants,' Diya said as she watched Hathi anxiously. The elephant was still spooked by whatever had been in the bushes and hadn't approached the water.

'Well, whatever it was, it has gone for now,' said Mak firmly. 'Let's not hang around here any longer than we need to. He pointed his spear upstream. 'Let's go.'

He led the way along the shore, alert for any threats the jungle might throw at them. His dream of escaping into the jungle felt soured after that shock, and now all he wanted to do was get Hathi back home . . .

Then he could think about returning himself.

CHAPTER TWELVE

Following the river was easier said than done. The sandy banks didn't last for long. When they met a sharp bend, the ground rose where the river had eroded it, becoming more treacherous.

They saw several huge water lizards basking in the trees above the river, their thick black forked tongues constantly tasting the air. Some were much bigger than Mak, and he wondered if that's what had stalked them earlier. The reptiles seldom attacked people, but Diya's stories had spooked him . . .

Giving the lizards a wide berth, they pressed on. Reaching the river bend, the bank became fragile and crumbled under Hathi's weight – sending large chunks of earth into the water and startling the elephant so much that he retreated to safer ground. There he refused to move for an hour while Mak tried to coax him onwards.

The crumbly terrain had forced them away from

the water into the trees. Without a well-trodden track to follow, their progress slowed. After several more hours, the trees had become noticeably denser, their lofty canopies blotting out the sun and turning the ground into a murky twilight that was alive with insects. With each step, it seemed as if the jungle was trying to pull them away from the water – which was the only point of reference Mak had to navigate them towards the elephant herd.

Eventually Diya threw her arms to the sky in despair. 'I'm exhausted!' Although used to the jungle, she'd never been in anything as dense. 'I need to stop.'

It was the fourth time she'd said it, and each time Mak had urged her a little further on. This time he thought it best to agree. Diya sat on a fallen log, took her pack off and tossed it to the ground.

Hathi seemed happy enough, nosing around some ferns hardy enough to grow on the darker forest floor. Mak sat on a stump at the edge of the clearing and took a swig from his water bottle. He only had a mouthful before it ran dry, and he suddenly regretted not finding a clear place to fill it near the river.

Diya spoke up. 'Don't take this the wrong way, Mak, but are you certain you know where we are?'

Mak took the satellite phone from her pack and sat back on his stump as he examined it.

'We don't need to know exactly where we are.' Mak saw the alarm on Diya's face. 'I mean, I know where we need to get to, and I know we're going the right sort of way by following the river.' He could tell Diya wasn't entirely pleased with that explanation.

She took a sweet trail bar from her pack and bit into it thoughtfully as she regarded Hathi.

'It's just that each step feels like we are getting more and more committed to the route,' she said. 'And I really don't want us to make a mistake and anything to happen to either us or Hathi . . .' Her voice tailed off.

'Nor do I, Diya, but if you don't take any risks in the jungle, you die. My time when I was lost taught me that.'

Diya smiled at him.

'And poor Hathi.' She paused, swatting a wasp away from her. 'I mean, every encounter he's had with people has been horrible. Captured by loggers. Hurt by Buldeo and those horrible men. Yet see him now – he trusts us.' Hathi's trunk delicately picked the fronds from a plant, leaving the stem intact. 'He knows we're trying to help him.' She paused again. 'I guess if he trusts you, so do I. Elephants are incredibly intelligent. My father thinks they're far smarter than we are.'

Before Mak could react, the log under Diya shifted with the sound of breaking damp wood, and Diya jerked downwards a few centimetres, her arms flailing to catch her balance.

She broke into nervous laughter. 'I think this log is rotten!'

Mak jumped to his feet and held up his hand. 'Stay where you are.'

'I don't—'

'Don't move,' said Mak urgently. 'The log is about to break open.'

‘So?’

‘So . . . there’s a massive wasps’ nest inside it . . .’

For Diya, it was as if the volume around her suddenly raised on cue. She thought she’d been swatting the occasional annoying wasp attracted to the sweetness of her trail bar, but now she saw the log around her was humming with small bodies as they poured from cracks along the trunk. One part of the wood had caved in so badly that she could see a damaged papery nest within, and countless wasps dashing to repair the breach.

Living in the jungle for most of her life meant Diya was not the sort of person to feel squeamish around insects, but she also knew that a swarm of angry wasps was not just bad . . .

It was deadly.

Then with a loud dull crack, the log gave way completely from under her.

CHAPTER THIRTEEN

A black cloud of smoke erupted from the broken log and encompassed Diya. Mak saw her tumble backwards before losing sight of her.

'Diya!'

He rushed forward, unsure what to do. Then Diya burst from the swarm, screaming at the top of her lungs.

She raced towards Mak, and the swarm behind her coiled in pursuit, thousands of tiny beating wings creating a drone so loud that Mak could feel it vibrating in his ribcage.

'Follow me, Diya!' Mak screamed. And with that he started to run.

He'd instinctively chosen a direction in which to sprint and only hoped it was towards the water, the one place he could think of that might save them from the angry wasps. Ahead, their path was barred by thick vines and creepers, which threatened to ensnare them. Even the machete wouldn't open the trail fast enough to save them.

But Hathi could.

The swarm triggered a primeval response of terror in the calf. No matter how big an elephant was, a horde of stingers could still be lethal. Hathi hadn't been too close to Mak or Diya when the log broke, but now he was powering ahead of them at incredible speed. With a slight tilt of his head, Hathi struck the natural barrier.

The plants didn't stand a chance in the way of a stampeding elephant. They tore like paper as Hathi bulldozed through them. Mak and Diya followed the elephant calf as close as they dared, fearful of being trampled, but despite their caution they were still running flat out to keep up.

Behind, the swarm snaked effortlessly through the obstacles and was catching up.

They had no choice but to keep running. Mak remembered a nature documentary that said swatting a wasp made it excrete chemicals that encouraged the rest of the swarm to attack. If that happened, it would be carnage.

Diya stumbled on a crooked root and was propelled forward, half falling, half running. Mak had already adjusted his stride, ready to backtrack to help her up, even though it might end up

getting them both murderously stung.

He wasn't really looking where they were going – until a mighty splash from ahead drenched him with water. He skidded in the mud, trying to slow down, only to see that Hathi had led them straight into the river – and then he fell in head first himself.

The cool water enveloped Mak, and he accidentally swallowed a mouthful of brown muck before surfacing. His feet touched the mud beneath and he was able to steady himself in time to see Diya complete her jungle dash with a desperate leap into the water. Hathi stood up to his belly and used his trunk to spray a curtain of water at the wasp cloud.

A few brave insects tried to get close, but soon retreated with the majority of the swarm. They circled the bank, then disappeared back into the gloom of the forest, their ominous droning fading into silence.

Mak took a deep breath, then met Diya's gaze. It rapidly changed from fear to relief at their lucky escape. Mak waded over to Hathi and patted the elephant on his neck.

'Well done, Hathi! You saved us!'

Hathi responded by playfully squirting water over him. Mak laughed and slapped water over the elephant, triggering an impromptu water fight.

'See?' said Diya, joining in the battle. 'I told you elephants could smell water!'

It was a few minutes before their elation wore off and Mak realized he no longer had his satchel over his shoulder.

'No!' he shouted. 'It's gone! My satchel.' He stared downriver but couldn't see any sign of it. Somehow it must have got ripped off him as he'd skidded into the river.

They both searched for a good hour, but to no avail. Mak realized that his machete was also missing, along with at least half of their provisions, the torches and the water purifier.

'It's a disaster,' Mak mumbled to himself.

Luckily, though, the one thing they hadn't lost was the satellite phone, which had been fixed on to a separate strap round Mak's belt. But it was soaking wet and failed to turn on when he pressed the power button.

'I guess it's time to test your survival skills, Mak,' Diya said with a deep sigh. 'We'll be OK. Don't worry.'

He didn't reply, and she put a hand on his shoulder to comfort him.

CHAPTER FOURTEEN

Mak made rapid progress up the tree.

His hands easily found nooks in the bark, while his bare toes gripped round every knot and branch. The moment he'd taken off his shoes and scrunched his toes in the soft dirt, he'd felt a tingle of familiarity course through his body.

It was as if it were only yesterday that he'd been barefoot and racing through the jungle.

They'd left the water and moved further up the riverbank until they found the tallest tree on their side of the river.

Mak had encouraged Diya to join him, but with a shake of her head she muttered that she'd rather have her feet firmly on the ground. The old tree's trunk was enormous and so craggy that scaling it wasn't too much of a problem.

During his ascent, Mak could see nothing but the mass of thick branches below, or the occasional glimpse of a wall of green from the tree opposite. There was no sense of how high he was, until he finally pulled the thinning upper branches away and was rewarded with a breathtaking vista of the forest.

It was a carpet of green that undulated over gentle hills stretching in every direction. They were covered in a fine cotton-wool veil of moisture-heavy clouds formed by the breathing trees themselves. Clouds that threatened to unleash a torrent of rain.

Mak took in the brown river that curved like a spine through the trees. It made it easy for him to pinpoint their location on the map, imprinted in his memory. Keeping one hand firmly on the thinning trunk, and his toes gripping the branch, he slowly twisted round as he zeroed in on a distant valley. It was the start of the hill range that eventually tapered into the valley on the map, the place through which the elephant herd would be passing. Even from here he could see some of the hills were more like miniature limestone mountains, cutting above the jungle.

'I can see the hills!' he called down to Diya.

She shouted something in return, but her voice was muffled by the dense branches of the trees.

'What?' shouted Mak.

Again, her reply was inaudible.

Mak was enjoying the gentle breeze on his face

and felt reluctant to drop back down into the humid jungle. He was positioning himself for a rapid descent through the branches when something caught his eye.

A distinctive line of smoke.

Nothing more than a thin vertical smudge against the sky, the top of which was whisked away by the breeze. But it was definitely man-made – a campfire.

And a quick calculation confirmed that it was in the direction from which they had come . . .

'Somebody is following us,' said Mak the moment he'd bounced down the tree. He'd descended with such carefree abandon that Diya had thought he'd fallen. He dropped the last metre or so next to her in a shower of leaves.

'Who?' she asked, looking around as if half expecting somebody to walk through the trees to greet them.

Mak took the sat phone from his bag and tried it once more. It was still dead. 'Best case is that it's our parents, tracking us down.'

Diya shivered at the thought. 'If that's the best case, then do I want to hear the worst?'

Mak couldn't bring himself to say, but a quick glance towards Hathi was all he needed to do to confirm Diya's suspicions.

'We need to be sure whether or not we're being followed by Buldeo. If we are, then it changes everything.' He paused. 'After all, it could just be loggers.' Even as he said the words, he didn't really believe it. They hadn't come across anything that resembled a track the loggers would use to access the heart of the jungle.

On Mak's last adventure, he'd experienced a run-in with poachers, though, so he had first-hand knowledge about how ruthless such men could be.

They needed to find out if it was either their parents, loggers or Buldeo himself.

'You can wait here for me to find out, Diya. It won't take me long.'

Diya frowned as he began walking away. 'Where are you going?'

'I can move quicker on my own,' said Mak. 'At the pace we've been walking, I reckon they're only about an hour behind us. They must have set off at dawn to catch up with us. Besides, you need to look after Hathi. I promise I won't be long.'

'Makur! Little Wolf!' Diya called after him. 'You've forgotten your shoes!' But he'd already disappeared into the thick undergrowth. She shook her head. 'I'm sure that boy is half monkey . . .'

CHAPTER FIFTEEN

The whipping branches were close enough to take Mak's ear off. But, with his head bowed, he didn't flinch as he powered through the thick forest.

Running barefoot was painful at first. The hardened callouses that he'd developed last time in the jungle had softened in the weeks after his return to civilization. However, he soon forgot the discomfort and ache in his legs as he leaped over roots and bounced across moss-covered rocks. He was loving every moment of it too much to care about the pain.

Doubling back the way they'd come, Mak kept close to the river, memorizing each bend so he knew just when to break away towards the smoke.

The last thing he wanted to do was run straight into a wolf or leopard, so he made no effort to mask the sound of his movement, knowing that it would frighten off any potential wild threat lurking ahead.

Only when he reached a specific bend in the river, with a steep, high bank on one side, did Mak start to disguise the sounds of his progress.

He'd noticed the steep drop-off into the river from his viewpoint at the top of the tree he'd climbed.

He was getting close.

Mak stopped to catch his breath. He was just able to smell the distinctive odour of smoke now through the jungle, betraying the campsite.

Mak crouched low and edged through the foliage with stealth, making as little noise as possible. He wondered if it really could be his parents, so angry that he'd disappeared again that they'd braved the jungle to find him and bring him home, kicking and screaming.

Would they think saving Hathi was a good enough reason not to punish him? After all, how different was that from what Diya's father was doing? Saving Hathi was simply extreme conservation.

His heart hammered in his chest as he became aware of indistinct voices ahead. He realized he was suddenly more afraid of his parents sending him back home and forbidding him from ever coming back to India than he was of bumping into a party of bloodthirsty poachers. He'd beaten poachers before. He never won any argument with his parents.

The smell of the campfire caught his nostrils and

Mak shot a hand across his stomach as it grumbled loudly.

That would be a stupid way to get caught, he thought to himself.

Dropping to all fours, Mak crawled forward, keeping his head low and his body just above the detritus on the floor. He headed for cover behind a broad tree and peeked through a bush.

Ahead was Mak's worst nightmare.

It was Buldeo and his two henchmen sitting round a campfire talking quietly.

Mak's heart fell. As soon as he saw their guns, he changed his mind about his parents. They were tough, for sure, but however angry they might be they wouldn't try to kill him. Buldeo, he wasn't so sure about. He felt a sharp stab of fear in the pit of his stomach.

The three men were just finishing off eating a bird they'd cooked over the fire.

'This stupid elephant better be worth it,' growled Lalu, who was already wiping his greasy fingers on his trousers and gathering his gear together.

Buldeo spat a bone into the fire. 'You'd rather head back to the city and get a labouring job? Work on a construction site again? Not me. Not again. That elephant is the key to my fortune.'

'*Our* fortune,' said Girish.

'That's what I said,' snapped Buldeo.

Lalu then stood and started circling the clearing. Three tents had been set up, and the men's backpacks hung from a tree at head height to keep them safe from insects and scavenging animals on the ground.

Mak noticed that Lalu's eyes were fixed to the ground, searching for something. He moved in a slow arc, drawing nearer to Mak's hiding place.

Closer . . .

Mak held his breath as Lalu walked slowly towards him, stopping just a couple of metres away. He knelt down, using his rifle for support. Mak could see the pockmarks in the man's skin and his chipped and crooked yellowing teeth. Lalu slowly raised his head and looked straight in Mak's direction.

Every muscle in Mak's body tensed as he prepared to run . . .

'Hey!' Lalu said. 'I've got something.'

Mak had no doubt he could outrun the men, but their guns . . . that was another matter. It seemed as if Lalu was looking straight at him, but the man didn't make any move to grab him.

'I found the trail again. The elephant trampled through the mud here. The tracks aren't old. Maybe half a day, if that. Could even be just a few hours. It's difficult to be precise.'

Mak gently released the breath he had been

holding. Lalu obviously couldn't see him hidden in the dense undergrowth, and he was further camouflaged by the low light under the canopy.

'Do we stand a chance of getting him tonight before he makes it back to his herd?' Buldeo asked.

Lalu ignored the question. 'There's something else here,' he replied.

From his position, Mak could see Lalu run a finger through the mud. He was tracing the outline of a very distinctive human footprint.

Lalu slowly pulled his rifle level as he turned back to Buldeo. 'We've got more human ones again, boss. Clearer this time.' He paused and looked around. 'Our elephant definitely didn't escape. He was *stolen*.'

Lalu stood up and menacingly chambered a round in his rifle.

The mission had just changed . . .

CHAPTER SIXTEEN

Mak's blood ran cold. He was convinced Lalu was going to lunge for him. Instead, the man hawked and spat in the ground before returning to the camp.

Still on all fours, Mak slowly retreated towards the water, his mind racing.

The men now knew about Mak and Diya. It wasn't as if they had been making any attempt to hide their tracks, so they would be easy to follow. Not only that, three men on foot would move quicker than he and Diya leading an elephant.

He had to find a way to stall them.

His hand slipped into his pocket and he felt the reassuring hilt of his penknife. He looked around for inspiration . . . How could he slow them down with just a few trees and a river? It was impossible.

Impossible . . . It was a word he knew well. People called his magic illusions impossible. He'd heard his survival alone in the jungle had been impossible. And yet . . .

Mak smiled as a plan slowly began to form in his head.

Aware that Buldeo and his men were still close, he crawled towards a willow drooping over the river a little further downstream. Its branches were laden with thick vines that were slowly suffocating the tree, and trailing a good ten metres in length.

Shimmying up the curved trunk, Mak opened his penknife and began hacking at the vine. Even the razor-sharp blade had trouble cutting through the fibres, but he managed to furiously saw through a dozen of them. They fell, coiling in the sand below.

He jumped down and gathered the vines over his shoulder. Already he was sweating from the effort, his shirt sticking to him. But he had no time to lose – he had to enact his plan before Buldeo dismantled the camp.

Mak carefully moved back upstream next to the camp. He then knelt on the raised riverbank and peered over the edge. It was a good twenty-metre drop down to the water below.

He carefully knotted the vines together to make a single long rope. As he did so, he caught sight of movement in the river as a huge crocodile broke the surface, its head almost as big as Mak's body.

He remembered reading somewhere that to estimate the size of a croc, you multiply the length of the head by seven. He imagined the length of the animal stretching underwater. It was enormous.

Big enough to eat him whole.

Or Buldeo.

Mak then fastened the end of the long vine around a small boulder he had spotted near the top of the bank. It was roughly the size of a big football.

Now came the dangerous part.

Walking as softly as he could, Mak sneaked back into the forest and began crawling towards the trackers' camp, gently uncoiling the rope behind him, making sure it didn't get tangled or wedged.

The three men were still talking loudly, but it was clear they were getting ready to leave.

Mak lay flat in the dirt and edged as close as he could, hidden from view by the tents. He then knotted the rope round two of the tent pegs before he reached the men's hanging backpacks. He deftly ran the rope through their straps before securing the very end to the third tent.

But just then . . . SNAP! A dry twig under his foot sounded as loud as a firecracker in the jungle. Buldeo, Lalu and Girish all spun round to face Mak – who, as luck would have it, was hidden from view behind a tree.

'What was that?' Buldeo grunted.

Mak froze. If he made a move, he'd be spotted. He couldn't see the men, but clearly heard the cold metallic click of Lalu's hunting rifle as they stood up.

The muffled clump of footsteps slowly approached . . .

Just as they were about to reach Mak's hiding place, there was the loudest squeal as a small Moupin pig burst from the undergrowth just in front of the men and charged across the campsite. There was a holler of surprise from the three men as the animal sprinted past them.

Mak peeked from behind the tree. The men had all spun round to follow the pig. Lalu already had his gun raised, aiming at his fast-moving target.

Mak sprinted for cover into the forest as the first gunshot rang out.

He reached the riverbank in seconds, and was relieved to hear the squealing pig was still alive and well as it vanished into the jungle. The sound of laughter from the men soon followed.

'You won't be laughing in a second,' Mak muttered as he took position next to the boulder he'd tied the rope to.

Bracing his back against a tree, he pushed with all his might. The rock began to roll across the earth. Another push, his leg muscles aching in protest – then the boulder toppled and started to roll down, eventually dropping off the edge of the steep-sided bank.

The boulder yanked the rope taut.

Mak hopped aside as the vine rushed between his feet. Back in camp, the vine had ripped the tents violently from the ground. Mak noted the distinct clank of equipment as their backpacks were also torn from the tree.

He dived for cover as he heard the rock splash down into the river – startling the crocodile, which powered across the water, leaving a mighty wake behind it.

Moments later, the tents and backpacks came rushing through the trees and over the edge – before splashing into the river below.

Mak crouched low in the bushes and tried to make himself as small as he could. And watched.

Within seconds, the three men burst out of the trees, swearing as their gear either sank into the murky depths or got taken rapidly downstream.

Girish dived from the steep bank and into the water without a thought.

Buldeo spotted the crocodile immediately. 'Girish, you fool! Get out!'

The huge reptile arced in the water and raced towards him like a torpedo. Mak felt a surge of panic. All he'd wanted to do was delay the men, not get them killed.

Girish was a strong swimmer and quickly turned round and clambered up the bank, gasping for breath. Buldeo and Lalu ran to help him – just as the crocodile burst from the water in a colossal explosion of water.

The three men howled in terror and fled in separate directions back into the trees.

The enormous crocodile pursued Girish for a few metres up the bank before giving up and circling back to the water.

The last thing Mak saw before he melted into the jungle was the crocodile's jaws chomping down on the one remaining backpack, floating in the river. And then the croc began violently shredding it to bits.

CHAPTER SEVENTEEN

It was Hathi who sensed somebody was approaching long before Diya heard the gentle rustle of branches. Mak jogged into the clearing feeling exhausted but thrilled. He'd been able to follow Hathi's path back to Diya, grinning all the way about his trap having worked so well.

He'd paused several times in an attempt to conceal their previous tracks, hoping that Lalu would be thrown off their scent once he recovered from the crocodile incident, but he wasn't so sure how effective his efforts had been. He quickly filled Diya in on what he'd seen and done.

'Do you think they'll continue following us, even without their equipment?' she asked with concern.

That had been weighing on Mak's mind during his trek back.

'I think Buldeo is desperate enough. We may have gained several hours' head start, maybe even half a day.' He patted Hathi's flank. The little elephant gave a tiny trumpet of acknowledgement before resuming plucking leaves from a tree. 'But, either way, this big lug is slowing us down.' He lapsed into a thoughtful silence. 'I thought we'd be much quicker than this.'

'If we knew exactly where the herd is, perhaps we could find a shortcut to them?'

'Good idea, but the phone doesn't work.' Mak sighed. 'We'll have to stick to the plan or we'll risk taking a wrong shortcut and carrying on right past them.'

'Rice?' Diya held up a silver bag. It was one of the vacuum-packed bags she'd kept in her trouser pockets, and one of the only bits of her gear that hadn't been lost in the river. Mak reached over for it, his stomach rumbling.

'Thanks! I'm starving.' He opened the seal and popped his fingers inside, hoping to find some hot rice. Instead he found a phone. He slowly pulled it out and looked quizzically at Diya. 'Very funny.'

Diya rolled her eyes and took the phone off him. 'Rice is super-absorbent. If you drop your phone in a puddle –' she turned the satellite phone on, and Mak was surprised to see the display light up – 'then the rice helps dry it out!'

Mak took the phone and used it to playfully prod

Diya in the arm. 'If you're not careful, I may start thinking you're a genius!' He pointed across the clearing. 'The ground starts to rise in that direction. In about an hour we'll be higher and might get a good signal.'

He automatically turned the phone off again to save the battery.

Diya was already walking. She glanced over her shoulder. 'What are you waiting for, then?'

They followed a well-worn animal trail, which gently snaked uphill for several miles. On the one hand, it meant they were making good progress, but on the other it also meant that if Buldeo was still following then he'd catch up with them quickly.

Mak guessed they'd reached the start of the limestone hills he'd seen from the top of the tree. On the map they had been nothing more than a dense mass of black contour lines, whereas in reality they were steep hills – sheer cliffs in some cases – that rose hundreds of metres from the jungle floor.

The dense foliage eventually fell away to one side, offering a breathtaking view across the jungle. They were well above the trees and could see a gentle blanket of grey mist closing in, blotting the treetops as it moved. It turned the sunshine hazy, almost dreamlike.

Mak was captivated and could have stared at it for hours, but Hathi nudged him in the back to return him to the moment.

With a nod, Mak then turned the phone on and thumbed through the onscreen options. He dialled his sister's number reluctantly. A quick look at his watch showed him that they had two hours before sunset. They obviously wouldn't be back at base camp tonight.

His sister warily answered the phone.

'Hello?'

Mak put on a cheery carefree voice. 'Hey, sis. It's Mak!'

'Makur! Where the heck are you guys?' Her tone warned Mak that something was wrong. 'You're in big trouble!'

CHAPTER EIGHTEEN

For a moment Mak thought Anula knew they'd freed Hathi, but then he remembered his sister had a habit of blowing everything out of proportion, especially if she *had* been getting some aggravation from their parents.

'Oh, we're still near the hide, looking across at the trees,' Mak said as casually as he could. A flock of parrots swooped noisily past, their feathers a kaleidoscope of colour as the sun reflected off their wings. 'And there are some amazing parrots here.'

'You're *still* birdwatching?' Anula asked suspiciously.

'Of course. You should come and join us. It's amazing out here.' Mak was confident that his sister would react badly to the suggestion.

'Like I'd want to do that!'

The little victory made Mak smile. 'We popped back to camp earlier to grab something to eat.'

Anula paused, as if assessing just how true that was. 'Did you see Mum and Dad?'

'No. What were they doing today?'

'They went with Anil to get some supplies. They were looking for you.'

Mak could barely contain his relief, but spoke as casually as he could. 'Oh, that explains why I couldn't find them. Tell them we were looking for them, and we're staying out again as Diya's getting lots of rare sightings out here.'

'Well, I think you should come back now, Makur.

Otherwise I am the one who ends up in trouble.'

'We will. Of course. Soon.'

He needed a change of tack.

'By the way, we were supposed to check on the herd's location.'

'Well, when you get back—'

'We were supposed to do it earlier and forgot because we were, um, looking for Mum and Dad. And you know Anil – he'll be disappointed with Diya if he thinks she's put birdwatching before the elephants.' He knew his sister would be more sympathetic if Diya was in trouble rather than him.

'All you have to do is check the monitors and let us know where they are, so if he asks us when we get back . . .' He glanced at Hathi, who was taking the opportunity to throw some dust over his back to cool off, and suddenly felt inspired. 'I mean, we wouldn't want anything to happen to the herd just because we forgot to check them, would we?'

He knew it was the perfect reasoning. Despite her attitude, he knew Anula was an animal lover.

'Hold on, then,' she said with reluctance. He heard her leave the cabin and walk across the camp. There were a few clicks as she turned the monitors on. Then she finally spoke up. 'I see them. They look fine to me.'

'And the map . . . ?'

'Oh yeah . . .'

'What?'

'They've changed direction.'

Mak could hear the clicking of the mouse. His sister might be a number of things, but she was far more competent on the computer than he was. He tried to imagine the map in his mind's eye.

'OK, they've turned twenty-three degrees south. It looks like they're avoiding some nasty hills. But . . .'

Mak nervously paced as Anula lapsed into silence. He was about to check they were still connected when she spoke again.

'It looks like they're heading straight for a village.'

Mak frowned. 'A village?' He pictured the map in his head and knew exactly where that was. It was a small settlement, populated by local farmers.

'That's good, then . . . ?' Anula queried.

Mak saw a horrified look on Diya's face. He covered the phone as Diya whispered to him.

'They are heading towards the village? That's awful news!'

'Why?' Then as an afterthought he spoke into the phone. 'Hold on, sis.' He pressed the mute button.

'I've been to the village with my father. The farmers hate the elephants. They think the animals threaten their crops. And we also think that the loggers have been taking them out using the roads they've been carving through the jungle.' She paused. 'It means the elephants are targeted by both loggers and villagers. If the herd goes there, they'll be in big trouble.'

She looked sadly at Hathi, who was oblivious to the seriousness of their conversation.

'My father has tried to work with the villagers to build fences to keep the elephants away. We've had some success, but they always said they would kill the elephants if they came back to the village. And they mean it.'

'The entire herd is heading in their direction!' Mak said with concern.

Diya nodded sadly. 'The farmers will shoot them.'

CHAPTER NINETEEN

After quickly hanging up the sat phone, Mak and Diya agreed to press on as far as they could. They needed to put as much distance as possible between them and Buldeo before the light failed. It was one thing being pursued by the bad guys, but now they also had to rush to stop the herd from running into a deadly trap.

The track ahead sloped back down as they crossed a limestone ridge, and from somewhere ahead they could hear the sound of running water.

'I don't think it's the same river as before,' said Mak, remembering the map's network of smaller tributaries that weaved through the jungle. 'And I don't think we should get too close to it now that it's getting darker.'

They stopped to bed down for the night and felt an intense thirst overwhelm them after marching so hard in the intense humidity without much rest.

They'd been sweating heavily with every step, almost all day. Before entering the thickest part of the jungle, they'd used the last of Diya's water, and now dehydration was catching up with them.

Mak knew they could go without food for days, but water was essential. They looked at Hathi, who was quite content drinking murky water from a muddy pool.

'The water purifier was in the pack.' Mak sighed.

Diya held up her finger towards the sound of rushing water. 'What about that?'

Mak pulled a face. 'The light's fading, so we wouldn't be able to judge if it is safe from any crocs, never mind drinkable.'

'So we die of thirst in the rainforest?'

Mak waved his fingers like a magician. 'I can make water appear out of nowhere!'

Diya looked expectantly at his empty hands. 'That was a terrible trick.'

Laughing, Mak shook his head. 'The moisture from fruits will help for now. We'll survive.' He winked and headed deeper into the forest.

After a few minutes of foraging, he returned with armfuls of papaya fruit.

'Now let's tuck in.'

They ate the fruits in pleasant silence, throwing a few to Hathi, who ate them whole. They looked longingly at the bag of rice that Diya had kept the sat phone stowed in, but Mak insisted they didn't light a fire in case it alerted Buldeo to their location.

The lack of fire soon brought problems of its own as the fog they'd seen earlier finally caught up with them, laying wispy tendrils down between the trees and causing the temperature to drop until they were both soon shivering.

Mak stood and paced around in an effort to warm himself up. 'We should make sure we don't get any unwelcome visitors tonight.' With his penknife, he cut more vines from the trees. 'I'm going to set up a perimeter!' He yanked a vine down from a tree. 'An early warning in case Buldeo and his goons decide to pay us a visit during the night.'

The thought of that frightened Diya. She nodded. 'Good idea.'

Since encountering poachers last time he was in the jungle, Mak had read up about the snares and traps they used. He had no intention of constructing anything that would hurt an innocent animal, but something noisy that would alert them to unwelcome snoopers would be ideal.

Mak wound the vine round their camp, at shin height, going from tree to tree in a large circle.

The vine acted as a basic tripwire across every approach to their camp. Mak then unscrewed the metal mug from his water bottle and filled it with small stones. He placed it at arm's reach up in a tree, balanced in the crook of a branch. Then he attached a small bit of vine from the cup to the main tripwire.

If anyone triggered the tripwire, it would pull the metal mug full of stones off the branch and come clattering down on to the rock floor below, making one hell of a noise.

Perfect, thought Mak.

Turning his attention to their camp, he selected a spot among the roots of a tree. He checked that there were no burrows from any animals that might want to bite them during the night, and then swept the area for nasty insects or snakes.

Breaking off some branches, he covered the area with armfuls of broad leaves to form a basic mattress, which would also give them some warmth. Then he used more leaves and branches to create a basic overhead cover for them. It was simple, but would help them to stay dry.

Standing back, he looked at his temporary camp.

He turned to Diya. 'The best way to stay warm is, um, for us to share body warmth,' he said awkwardly.

Diya said, 'OK, then. I'm tired already.'

She settled down in the basic shelter and, after a few moments, Mak joined her.

He looked up at their rooftop of branches and gently turned his back to Diya.

'Try to sleep. Tomorrow will be a big day. For us and for Hathi.' He paused. 'And well done today. It is nice being together on this mission. We are a good team, eh?'

'Yes. A good team. Sleep well, jungle boy!'

He felt her turn and press against his back as well, and immediately he felt warmer.

Mak thought he'd stay awake the whole night, but swiftly found sleep embracing him. He was so tired, it felt as if he was sinking into the ground . . .

CHAPTER TWENTY

Mak jerked awake suddenly. The feeling of sinking had been so intense that he'd dreamed he was wading through quicksand – but now he was instantly alert, his senses sharp.

What had woken him? Had a tripwire been triggered?

He heard Diya's steady rhythmic breathing behind him, the gentle grumbling from Hathi and the river, which sounded louder in the dead of night. Nothing was amiss, yet something had disturbed him.

Gently pushing aside the branches of their makeshift roof, and taking care not to wake Diya, Mak clambered outside. The mist spiralled through the trees, and the reflecting moonlight gave the impression that the ground was glowing.

He headed straight for Hathi, who was peering into the darkness, ears cocked for any sound. The elephant ran his trunk across Mak as he gently patted the animal and spoke in a low voice.

'What's the matter, Hathi? Is someone out there?'

He doubted Buldeo would have caught up with them in the dark, especially with most of their equipment at the bottom of the river, and he suspected a leopard or tiger would alarm Hathi, whereas the elephant seemed more curious than frightened.

Then the loggers' tales of killer crocodiles and enormous snakes came to mind, and Mak wished Diya hadn't mentioned them. Although he'd survived the jungle before, it was still easy to believe that something *unknown* lurked out there, waiting to be discovered.

Mak edged further into the trees, mindful not to trigger his own traps. Then he stopped in his tracks as he heard a great crashing of branches. The mist swirled and a giant loomed into view. Mak's heart pounded, his legs twitched ready to run, but his instincts kept him rooted to the spot.

It looked like a buffalo, but much larger, standing almost twice as tall as Mak. Huge horns curved from an unusually high ridge on the animal's head. Its powerfully built body was covered in black fur, while its legs looked as if it was wearing white socks.

It flared its ears, each as big as Mak's hand, as it studied him.

Mak had no doubt he could be trampled to death by this huge creature.

Six more animals appeared, but they were more interested in eating than they were in Mak. He flinched when Diya suddenly appeared behind him, whispering softly.

'Cool, eh? They are gaur. The largest cattle in the world.' She stood next to him, gazing at the animals in wonder as they spread out around them. The bull snorted, then resumed eating as it judged the children were no threat. 'There are not that many of them left. We're lucky to see them here.'

They watched the gaur spread out through the mist, communicating with occasional dull grunts and barely making a sound as they rummaged through the undergrowth. The mist gave the scene such a dreamlike quality that Mak had to pinch himself to check he was still awake. The huge beasts eventually disappeared into the darkness, leaving Mak and Diya breathless with wonder.

'That was awesome!' said Mak.

Diya nodded. 'Good job your tripwires warned us of the danger,' she said sarcastically, nudging Mak in the arm and returning to their bivouac. Mak followed before wondering why the gaur hadn't tripped a single wire.

He was so wrapped up in his thoughts that he didn't notice his foot snagging the very vine he'd been thinking about. It yanked the smaller vine attached to the metal mug, and with a big clang it fell to the ground, scattering the stones across the rocks.

Mak's heart leaped, and then it jumped again as several birds that had been sleeping in the tree took to the air, squawking noisily.

CHAPTER TWENTY-ONE

By dawn, the mist had left every leaf in the forest dripping with dew, which Mak and Diya licked eagerly.

Mak smiled to himself – they were beginning to live like the animals of the jungle: surviving moment to moment, and using what nature provided.

Breakfast was formed of wild fungi and the few berries they found that Hathi hadn't yet eaten. Diya was particularly skilled at identifying the poisonous ones – plucking a berry or a mushroom out of Mak's fingers just as he was about to eat it.

The sun warmed the forest, and Mak, with a spring in his step, led the party towards the sound of roaring water. After a few hundred metres, their trail led straight to the top of a gorge where white water frothed fifteen metres below.

'Lucky we didn't stumble this way in the dark,' Mak said, looking down.

The pathway wound along the gorge and rapidly descended to the waterline. They took care as Hathi was clearly agitated by the height, and the last thing they needed was for the elephant to panic.

They were soon on a broad rocky shore that stretched away from the gorge. Here the water was no longer frothing and white, but it flowed quickly and disappeared round a bend where the dense jungle hung over the banks of the river.

Hathi trumpeted with delight and waded knee-deep into the water, splashing himself, then squirting water at the children.

'Cut it out!' said Mak, laughing hard.

Diya wasn't so amused. She was looking downstream. 'That terrain is going to slow us down,' she said.

Mak pointed directly across the river where the flat shore continued.

'We need to cross this river at some point, Diya.' He pointed. 'The village lies that way. I'm sure of it.'

'But how are we going to cross this? It's way too wide to make any form of bridge.' Diya kicked a piece of driftwood at her feet. 'Perhaps we could build a raft?'

Mak gave her a worried look. 'Last time I built a raft, I ended up nearly drowning. Trust me, it's not as easy as it looks. And building one to take the weight of an elephant . . .' He trailed off as he glanced upstream.

Diya followed his gaze and gripped his shoulder in alarm.

'Mak!'

In the distance, they could see three figures at the very top of the gorge. They were too far away for them to make out any details, but in Mak's mind there was no doubt that it was Buldeo, Lalu and Girish.

The pair watched as the three figures hurried across the horizon, and were then lost from view behind the rocks.

'Do you think they saw us?' Diya asked in a low voice.

'Two kids and an elephant on a beach?' said Mak drily. 'I think it's likely. Even if they didn't, they'll be down here in less than an hour. My booby trap obviously didn't slow them down enough.'

They looked back at the river. It was an enormous obstacle. Diya started to walk downstream. 'We don't have time to waste. Hathi! Come on, boy. We need to move now!'

The elephant replied with a trumpeting sound, but made no effort to leave the water.

'Hathi! Come on!' She gestured towards the trees ahead.

The elephant stepped a little further into the river. The water was now tickling his underbelly.

Mak waded into the water with his arms extended to try to usher Hathi in the right direction. 'Come on, buddy. We have to move now.' Hathi responded by spraying him with water. Mak sputtered, swiping the water away from his face. 'We don't have time to play games!'

Seeing Mak's problem, Diya waded in to help, holding her arms out to coax the elephant back to land. She clicked her tongue and whistled in a soothing manner.

'Come on, Hathi! Don't be a pain!'

Hathi stepped further into the river.

Mak lunged for him, accidentally urging him even further forward. With a groan of frustration, he got round the front of the little elephant and tried pushing him back towards the riverbank.

He might as well have been shoving a mountain, but then with a final bellow Hathi surged forward into the river again. He moved so suddenly that Mak fell face first into the water. He coughed and spluttered as he felt his legs sweep from under him and he bobbed along in the surprisingly strong current.

'Hathi!'

He'd expected Hathi to flounder in the water, but was astonished to see the little elephant was paddling effortlessly, his trunk held high out of the water like a snorkel. And he looked like he was having the time of his life!

Diya dived forward to catch up with them and watched with Mak as the elephant splashed further into the river. They both circled Hathi, watching in wonder.

'I can't believe he's swimming!' Mak yelled before a wave splashed over his head. He spat out a mouthful of water, then looked around. The surface was becoming choppy as they rounded the river bend.

Then, without warning, they all gained speed. Spinning round, they saw the water ahead was frothing angrily. The current, intensified, was now hurtling them along towards another sharp bend.

CHAPTER TWENTY-TWO

A vicious current snapped at Mak's leg and he felt himself yanked downwards. His arms crawled through the water as he fought to the surface. The one rule enforced in his mind was 'Don't panic!'

This wasn't the first time he'd been swept away in a river, and he knew it was easy to get disorientated underwater, but he kept his head and followed the path of bubbles upwards.

He caught a flash of Hathi's legs powerfully treading water, before he surfaced close to the elephant. The animal was trumpeting in alarm, but with his trunk held high, he was in no immediate danger of drowning.

Diya, however, was in deep trouble.

He saw her just metres away, spinning out of control in the water's fierce rip. It was pointless to call out to her. Instead Mak summoned all his energy and swam towards her in a powerful front crawl. He could feel the current pulling at him, but remained resolutely on course.

Reaching Diya, he swept his hand around her, clutching at the back of her collar. She thrashed wildly, trying to stop herself from being pulled under, unaware that Mak was holding her. He was now at risk of being punched in the face by her as she struggled. Knocking him out now would probably see them both dead.

Gripping her collar tightly, Mak kicked against the water as hard as he could, holding her at arm's length to avoid a flailing fist. The sudden yank and change of direction forced Diya on to her back and she stopped writhing when she realized she was being helped. As soon as she stopped struggling, her body naturally floated, making Mak's job a little easier . . .

But pulling a body through turbulent water wasn't easy!

With just one free hand to swim to safety, Mak headed towards the bank – or at least where he thought the bank was. Being so low in the river, all he could see were rolling white-capped waves around him. He pushed harder, his legs now numb from both the cold water and extreme effort.

Then Mak struck something he thought was a rock.

A familiar bellow assured him that it was Hathi. Mak reached out blindly, searching for the elephant's head. Water stung his eyes, but he managed to cling on to Hathi's neck.

With a final grunt of effort, he swung Diya around. She clambered up on to Hathi's back. The elephant grumbled, but the additional weight didn't seem to bother him. Diya spread herself flat, gasping for breath.

Mak slipped further into the river – only just grabbing Diya's boot before he could be swept away. Too exhausted to fight the current any longer, Mak floated and allowed the elephant to pull them along.

It seemed like an eternity before Mak felt the firm ground suddenly slap his backside as Hathi lumbered ashore. Mak rolled to his feet and crawled on to the rocks, gasping for breath. His legs felt like jelly, but his first concern was for his friends.

Hathi didn't look any worse for wear as he shook himself, sending a fine spray of water in the air. Diya had already slid from his back and was bent over, hands on knees, as she caught her breath.

'Are you OK?' Mak asked with concern.

They both looked back at the river. It was an undulating mass of frothing waves. They had crossed it while being swept along at a fast pace. The far bank was now a sheer wall of limestone, as tall as a tower block.

Further downstream, the river disappeared in a tight gorge. If Hathi hadn't made it to shore when he had, they wouldn't have survived.

Mak decided not to share that with Diya; he didn't see the point in frightening her. He expected her to be upset or afraid. Instead she looked at him with a broad smile and laughed out loud.

'That was amazing!'

Mak looked at her in confusion.

'It was exactly how I imagined whitewater rafting was going to be!'

Mak snorted with laughter, and with it coughed up a little of the river he'd accidentally swallowed. 'I think there are safer ways of doing it than riding on the back of an elephant!'

He looked upstream in the direction they'd travelled. Nothing looked familiar.

'We could have been carried half a kilometre. Maybe more,' he said.

Turning back to the jungle, he could just see distant slopes of limestone hills.

'We can use the sat phone to check our position,' Diya said, indicating Mak's belt.

He grabbed the pouch on his belt and opened it, relieved to see the phone was still safe in the sealed rice bag. He dried his hands by wiping them on tufts of grass before pulling the phone out and turning it on.

'It still works!' he said with relief as the display lit up.

And then he saw the battery icon. Last time they'd called his sister, it had been half charged, and now there was only a tiny fraction remaining.

'I think the water may have damaged the battery. We might only have enough power left for one more call.'

They exchanged a worried look. They knew now wasn't the time to waste their last chance.

Mak turned the phone off.

'The more distance we put between Buldeo and Hathi, the better. We have no idea how long it will take them to find a way across.'

They stared at the jungle ahead. Maybe it was because of their recent near-death experience, but the trees seemed darker, intimidating, as if they held secrets Mak and Diya should never try to discover.

They had no choice but to go through them.

CHAPTER TWENTY-THREE

The ominous jungle was getting more challenging with every step. There were no animal trails to follow now, meaning Mak and Diya were forced to carve their own way through the vegetation, which was more difficult without their axe. The ground began to rise, becoming increasingly rocky, with sharp limestone protrusions poking out from the earth.

Diya stood on the rocks, convinced that having something firm underfoot would make her progress easier. But they were slick with moisture and moss, and her boots were unable to grip.

She slipped twice, ripping her trouser leg and grazing her knee so badly it brought tears to her eyes. Mak rolled up the material so he could inspect the injury. It wasn't deep, but Mak could tell it hurt.

She began to lower her trouser leg. 'I'll be OK.'

Mak stopped her. 'I know, but we still need to

clean it.' He could see Diya was about to argue, so he quickly continued. 'If it gets infected, it could lead to a whole host of serious problems.' He paused. 'Although, typical. I brought a first-aid kit all the way from London, and when we actually need it we've lost it.'

Diya looked around at the plants. 'I know what we can use. Pick some leaves off that plant there.'

Mak moved to the small weed to which she was pointing. 'This? Are you sure?'

Diya nodded. 'It's plantago. Quite common.'

Mak passed her several leaves, which she chewed. She then spat out the mulch and kneaded it between her fingers, pausing only when she saw Mak's look of utter disgust.

'It's an antiseptic,' she said. She winced as she rubbed the oozy paste over the injury.

'It looks like it will kill anything,' Mak said, lips twisted in distaste.

He placed a leaf over the chewed gunk on her leg and secured it with a thin strand of vine. 'As good as new,' he said with a grin.

They studied the path ahead. The jungle canopy overhead was so thick that at times the ground seemed to be in perpetual night. Swarms of mosquitoes danced in the occasional shaft of sunlight that made it through. The rocks underfoot were so slick and jagged that nothing larger than moss could grow on them.

'There's no way Hathi can walk over that,' Diya said warily. 'Maybe we should turn round?'

'And head back to what?' Mak shook his head. '*This* is the only way forward. We're trapped by the river behind and every moment we waste—'

'Buldeo catches up,' Diya finished.

It was enough of a threat to force them onwards in silence. This time they allowed Hathi to lead. The elephant found the easiest path between the rocks as each step drew them gradually higher.

Through the trees they occasionally caught glimpses of a distant valley. Mak was starting to feel confident that they'd reached the start of Spiny Ridge.

'Are you sure you're remembering the map correctly?' Diya asked as they trudged behind Hathi.

Mak shrugged. 'I think so.' He paused, thinking. 'But then I get a bit nervous about how right I am. There weren't that many features on it, but the ones that were marked stood out. I'm hoping that once we reach the end of that ridge, it's downhill straight to the village.' He paused once more. 'The thing we don't know is whether or not we'll reach the herd before the farmers get to them.'

'We're running out of time. And if we get lost

between here and there . . .' Diya didn't want to finish that thought. If they got lost, took the wrong direction or became stuck, then there would be no way they could intercept the herd before they reached the village full of hostile farmers.

Mak knew that all too well, which was why he was insisting they press on with minimal breaks now. That in turn meant they hadn't eaten or drunk enough and were beginning to feel weak.

A short break in the trees offered them a sky that was a perfect orange as the sun set. The few clouds rippled with a red glow as if burning from the inside. It looked spectacular. Even Hathi gave a bellow of excitement.

They soaked up the sight for a moment, knowing that they would have to camp soon.

Mak then looked around and frowned when he spotted something in a tree.

'Hey. Look at that,' he said, taking a step closer. 'What is it?'

It looked like a large fruit hanging from the high branches – brown in colour, with a leathery skin that vaguely resembled a coconut. His stomach rumbled in anticipation. He stepped closer and realized the trees were full of them. He picked up a stone, intending to knock one down.

'Mak—!'

Diya's warning came too late. The stone was already out of his hand. It thumped hard into the branch just above his target.

The fruit didn't fall. Instead, it opened its wings and gave a high-pitched screech. It was a bat. The biggest bat Mak had ever seen.

Unfolded, its wingspan was almost as wide as the children were tall. Beneath was a skinny golden-furred body.

'Flying foxes!' Diya exclaimed as she tackled Mak

to the ground – and not a moment too soon.

The first bat launched itself from the tree and swooped low over their heads. Its sudden action startled the whole colony, which took to the air in a mass of screeching. Within seconds, the sky was black as hundreds of giant bats soared overhead, their leathery wings passing inches from the children lying on the ground with their arms covering their heads.

Hathi bleated in terror as the bats swarmed around him, his trunk waving frantically to swat them aside. The creatures were quick, but had no intention of attacking. They were fruit bats, disturbed by Mak, but searching for nothing more than a mango. Moments later, the air fell silent as the bats dispersed. Diya and Mak watched them soar like a smoke cloud, which then slowly vanished as the animals spread out to begin their nightly hunting.

Diya punched Mak in the shoulder. 'Maybe be a little more careful next time, eh, Mak?'

'Yes. Sorry,' he said sheepishly. 'I suppose I'd better prepare camp.'

CHAPTER TWENTY-FOUR

With the dense canopy smothering the light, night came quickly – and, with it, plunging temperatures. Mak and Diya sat together shivering against the chill and eating the few mushrooms they'd foraged along the way. There was nothing else to eat except a few insects, which Diya declined, but which Mak wolfed down.

'You really are becoming more jungle with every moment out here, Mak,' Diya said, wrapping her arms round her knees for warmth. 'Tell me those taste disgusting!'

'They taste disgusting!'

They both laughed.

Diya continued. 'We must be close to the herd by now.'

'Hopefully we'll find them by the end of tomorrow,' Mak said as he toyed with the sat phone. 'We can call my sister to check, if you like? But it will be the only call we'll be able to make. What if she doesn't answer? Should we maybe save it for an emergency?'

'Well, in most people's books, this is an emergency,' she replied. Then Diya gestured to the branches above them. 'Although we won't have a good signal under this. I think we'd better save the battery.'

Mak nodded and put the phone back in the rice bag. He was wondering if their parents had found out they were missing yet. Anula was a good liar, and he had no doubt she would say anything to get out of trouble, but . . .

'I don't know,' Diya said, as if reading his mind. 'We've been gone for two days already – my father will be worried.'

That had been weighing on Mak's mind too. 'I think I'm going to be grounded until I'm a pensioner,' he said shivering. 'I wish we had a fire,' he added, desperate to change the subject.

'I can make one,' said Diya.

Mak shook his head. 'We can't risk drawing attention to ourselves.'

Diya smiled and stood up, gathering dry twigs from the floor. 'Oh, Little Wolf. You still have so much to learn out here. The jungle has many more secrets to give. Let me show you *my* magic trick:

a covert fire.' She winked, giggling at the puzzled look on Mak's face. 'I will need you to dig a hole.'

She refused to answer any further questions, so Mak was left digging a half-metre-square hole in the ground as Diya gathered dry moss and kindling. Once she'd decided the hole was deep enough, Diya instructed him to dig a second, shallower hole about two paces away from the first. Cracking a sturdy branch from a tree, she used it to drive a tunnel in the ground between the two holes.

She leaned all her weight on the stick, pushing it through the bottom of the smaller hole at an angle, until the tip finally poked out into the bigger one.

'An underground chimney?' Mak asked puzzled.

'Kind of. But in reverse. When the kindling is lit at the bottom of this hole, oxygen will be sucked through here –' she indicated the tunnel – 'keeping it going longer.'

Mak watched in fascination.

'And because the fire is at the bottom of the hole, the flames are shielded from view. All you get is a bit of smoke out of the top.'

Using one of the waterproof matches from Mak's bag, she lit the fire. Sure enough, only a fine cloud of smoke rose from the pit. From where Mak was sitting, he couldn't even see the flames.

'That is awesome,' Mak said, impressed. 'Hathi, isn't that amazing?'

The elephant stood next to a tree, trying to sleep. He wagged his ears, totally unimpressed.

'That's not the impressive part,' Diya said proudly. 'Check this out.'

She stood up, reached past Mak for a small thorny shrub, and used Mak's penknife to cut the bark. A thick resin oozed out, which she caught in her hand.

'It's a guggul plant,' she explained. 'They use it in my village, if they can find it. It's getting quite rare, unless you are in deep jungle. The resin has amazing medicinal properties, and it also makes a very refreshing tea.'

The rest of the evening passed soaking up the warmth from the fire and enjoying the resin tea, which they heated in Mak's metal mug from his water bottle.

They were both left with a warm, fuzzy feeling in their stomachs.

Mak then had an idea and poured the open pack of rice into the boiling water. The food filled them up and sent a warm glow coursing through them.

They soon fell into a deep and restful sleep.

CHAPTER TWENTY-FIVE

They woke before the sun had risen. The sky cast a shadowless golden light over the landscape, giving a sense of peace. It was moments like this that reminded Mak just how beautiful the jungle could be.

They were both still full from the rice the night before and felt energized.

'This is it,' said Mak. 'This is the day we get you home.' He rubbed Hathi's trunk. He turned to Diya. 'Do you think we should try to call my sister now?'

Diya looked thoughtful. 'It's your decision, Little Wolf. But we might need her to guide us to the herd when we are closer. Don't forget that elephants are surprisingly stealthy. They could walk past us without us ever knowing.'

'She will go berserk that we haven't been in touch. That's going to waste a lot of battery life.' In his mind's eye, Mak could see his parents blowing their fuses as they searched for him. His idea to stay in touch every day had been a sensible one, but the jungle hadn't taken much notice of any of his best-laid plans.

Agreeing to leave the dreaded phone call until the very last moment, they continued along, reaching the edge of a clifftop.

The views were breathtaking. The mighty trees far below looked like nothing more than a canvas of broccoli, punctuated by columns of greyish limestone that rose out of the canopy like sentinels.

Mak pointed to a far ridge. 'I'm pretty sure that's Spiny Ridge . . .'

Diya raised an eyebrow. '*Pretty sure?*'

Mak ignored her. 'And there's the end of it, the V-shaped valley.'

Diya frowned. 'Are you sure that's the right direction?'

Mak pointed to the sun, then to the ridge. 'Look, according the sun's shadow, that is west-north-west. And that means over there should be the river.' He gently spun Diya round and was relieved to see a line meandering in the distant landscape. They were now high up enough to see not the river itself but just the dark gaps between the trees on either bank.

Diya nodded, impressed. 'Not bad.'

‘They don’t call me Big Wolf for nothing,’ Mak joked.

‘Correction. That’s why we call you *Little* Wolf.’ She smirked and continued walking on with Hathi.

The trees grew right up close to the edge of the cliffs. Some sprouted almost horizontally from the forest and hung precariously over the drop. That forced them to walk back into the denser jungle. The going was not as difficult as it had been, however, and after a couple of hours the path started to slope gently downwards.

The trees began to thin, and by the time they stopped for lunch, feasting on papaya and jackfruit, they’d reached a plateau offering a magnificent view ahead. They were still quite high up. Spiny Ridge was closer now, and the trail ahead wound through the rocks beyond. It was obviously man-made, a straight path forged through the dense undergrowth growing back over it.

Mak couldn’t hide the disappointment in his voice. ‘It looks like somebody has been here before us.’ He’d imagined them as pioneers, treading the unknown, but here was a clear sign they were not the first.

‘The villagers would probably venture out this far,’ Diya said quietly. ‘Even miners have travelled through this region in the past. They come out here searching for rare gems or minerals like coltan.'

'Coltan?'

Diya nodded. 'It's found mainly beneath jungles around the world, and it's worth more than gold. Tiny amounts are used in electronics. Your computers, televisions, games consoles – even the drone flying above our elephants – all use coltan in their components. The modern world may be a clever place, but unfortunately we are digging up the jungles like this to make it work.'

Mak felt sad at the thought that there was so much richness in the jungle that people were greedy for. It made him even more determined to stay and protect the jungle. It was worth fighting for.

They sat in thoughtful silence for several minutes watching a hawk soar below them on invisible thermal currents before it plunged downwards after its prey.

Then suddenly a sound drifted towards them from the distance. It was shouting.

Mak cupped his hands behind his ears and slowly turned his head. The action helped focus the sound, amplifying everything he heard. He'd almost turned a full one hundred and eighty degrees before the muffled sound of arguing became clearer. It was in Hindi, but the anger in the tone was unmistakable.

‘Buldeo?’ Diya whispered fretfully.

‘I’m not sure. I can’t make out the voices clearly enough. But they’re behind us, so I think we can bet that’s exactly who it is.’

Mak was annoyed at himself. Since crossing the river they hadn’t made any effort to conceal their tracks, which must have made Lalu’s life much easier. But it was too late to do anything about that now.

It was also hard to say how far away their pursuers were; sound could carry for miles in the valleys around them.

But one thing was for certain: they had to move quickly.

The race was on.

CHAPTER TWENTY-SIX

There was urgency with every step. This was not a time to be stealthy – it was about putting as much distance between them and Buldeo's gang as possible.

With each twist, the track hugged the side of the hill. Every so often, it would hook sharply round and they were greeted with a sheer cliff centimetres from their feet. At such drops Hathi would become noticeably more nervous, and he'd slow down.

Mak learned to distract the elephant by having several strips of succulent bamboo wedged in his belt with which to coax him.

The trail was becoming ever more treacherous, and they were still very high up. Mak was thinking about ways of getting further ahead of Buldeo when Diya suddenly shrieked and fell to the ground.

Mak ran to help her up.

'What happened? Are you OK?'

She winced as she rolled on to her back and sat up. 'My foot. I twisted it on that rock.' She indicated a gnarled stone that had tripped her.

Mak gently examined her foot and heard Diya murmur in pain. Her ankle was already swelling. 'Can you move it?'

Diya rotated it in an arc, wincing with pain. 'I don't think it's broken. Just twisted.'

She tried to stand, leaning on Mak's shoulder for support. When she put weight on her ankle, she sagged and dropped to her knees.

'I can't believe this.' She buried her head in her hands. 'What will we do if I can't walk?'

Mak looked back up the track, half expecting Buldeo to walk into view. 'We can't stop here.' He spoke softly. 'We need to think of something.'

'But I can't walk,' Diya whispered.

Mak felt a wave of panic. They'd got this far only to be sabotaged by a twisted ankle. He took a deep breath to calm himself. He knew that even the most minor injury could prove fatal in the wild. But he also knew that getting frustrated would achieve nothing. They needed a plan . . .

Hathi's trunk delicately nosed Diya's face as if sensing her pain. She patted him.

'Thank you, Hathi. I just need to rest it and not put weight on it.'

'Yes, you need to rest it,' said Mak, looking between Diya and the elephant. 'But Hathi is raring to go.'

'Then I could ride on his back,' said Diya excitedly. Mak looked uncertain. 'Come on, help me get up.'

Mak helped her stand. 'Are you sure?'

Hathi may be at ease around them, but he was still a wild animal. Buldeo hadn't managed to beat that out of him yet.

'Gently help me up. He won't mind.' Diya rubbed the elephant's back for emphasis.

As carefully as she could, Diya placed her arms over Hathi's neck and, with a boost from Mak, threw her injured leg over the animal. The elephant didn't seem to mind the extra load, and Mak fed him a piece of bamboo for good measure.

Diya shuffled forward so she was sitting over Hathi's front shoulders rather than on his spine. 'Do you know Indian royalty used to ride elephants?' she said in a posh voice.

Mak gave a mock bow. 'Your Majesty should twist her ankle more often, then. Come on, Hathi. Try not to drop her.'

The elephant followed Mak, and they were soon making swift progress again. Mak started to think

they might outrun Buldeo after all. But his building sense of excitement was suddenly extinguished when they heard shouting from behind.

'There they are!'

Buldeo, Girish and Lalu stood at the stop of the hill, silhouetted against the horizon. They were still some distance away, but their voices carried in the canyons.

'You little thieves! Stop right there!'

Mak flinched when they heard the distinctive

clap of a gunshot. He saw Buldeo swat Lalu's gun aside.

'You idiot! You'll hit the elephant!'

Then the trio vanished from view as they hurried in pursuit.

Mak had dived for cover behind a stout tree, and Hathi had half stumbled in fear of the sound, but Diya had held on tight.

'What do we do now?' Diya shouted down to Mak.

'We keep going. We never give up!'

And with that they pushed onwards and down into a narrow canyon.

But both of them got a sense that they were rapidly running out of time.

CHAPTER TWENTY-SEVEN

Mak's footsteps echoed in the rocky canyon, which constantly twisted and turned so they couldn't see what lay ahead. He'd coaxed Hathi into a run, and Diya was now desperately clinging on as each jolt threatened to knock her off. However, Hathi was not a quick creature, and Mak knew that the inevitable was looming.

Buldeo would eventually catch up with them.

He would catch them and take Hathi back to a life of imprisonment. And what would he do to the two witnesses? Nobody knew Mak and Diya were out here – not even their parents – and he doubted the men would risk a life behind bars by letting the children return to civilization to tell the authorities about Buldeo's cruelty. They'd already been shot at.

Buldeo could easily throw them off the edge of the cliff . . .

Mak needed more time. But that was impossible.

Unless . . .

He glanced ahead at the narrow canyon through which they were hurrying. Boulders and rocks had fallen at various times from the steep sides. Over the years, they had lodged against one another, turning a potential avalanche into a sturdy rock wall they were forced to squeeze past. It reminded Mak of a huge natural game of Jenga.

'Of course!'

He stopped Hathi and quickly looked around the canyon for anything that could assist him with his rapidly forming plan. Diya watched him, concerned.

'Why are we stopping?'

'Jenga!'

'What do you mean, Jenga? The game?'

Mak ran to a set of boulders and studied them. Thirty or more had fallen and were now wedged firmly on top of one another. Some were as big as a car, while others looked more manageable.

'I used to love it when I was a kid,' he muttered to himself. 'And I will love it even more if it slows those thugs down.'

'I don't understand.'

He leaned over and slapped his palm on one of the boulders. 'This is the one. If we move it, then the rock above it will move. If we're lucky, then the whole house of cards will come tumbling down.' He pointed out the precariously balanced rocks to Diya. 'Always the best bit of playing Jenga! Destroying the tower at the end!' He smiled.

Diya looked at him in disbelief. Then she looked at the stack of boulders. It was a lethal plan, one that could easily go wrong and crush them all to death.

But she also knew it was their only chance.

'How can we move something so heavy? Even with the two of us and Hathi, it can't be done.'

Mak was searching for something else now, waving his finger in the air as he did so. 'Then we need to be smart. That's what I learned from my magic tricks. Be smart and always remember KISS.'

'Kiss?'

'Keep it simple, stupid. And the simple solution is a lever.'

'We don't have a lever.'

Mak stopped and smiled at her. 'But you and the jungle have taught me that we can always make what we need.'

He gestured to a small tree attempting to grow from the side of the canyon wall. It was about twice his height and as thick as his leg. All he had to do was pull it down.

Mak flung his arms round the tree and pulled with all his might. It didn't budge.

'It's a tree . . .' said Diya, shaking her head.

Mak shifted position and pressed his back against the trunk. When it didn't move, he raised both legs against the cliff wall and pushed.

'It's not . . . breaking . . .' he wheezed through gritted teeth.

'Hathi. Over there! Come on, boy!' Diya gently coaxed the elephant, squeezing him with her heels as if he were a horse. Hathi approached the tree and watched as Mak tried once again to pull it over. Diya clung on to Hathi's back as, with a playful bellow, the elephant pressed his forehead against the trunk and pushed.

Mak was still hanging, propped between the wall and the tree, when it shuddered, the wood cracking as Hathi uprooted it, exposing a big clump of fat, tangled roots.

Mak tumbled, groaning, to the canyon floor.

Hathi's trunk snuffled Mak's face to check he was in one piece.

'I'm OK, pal,' he said, pushing the wet trunk aside. 'But a little warning would have been nice.'

Bent almost double, Mak dragged the little tree to the boulders he'd marked out. The tree was heavy and he was forced to roll it, using the roots as a pivot, as if wielding a giant mop, but he eventually managed it.

With a final grunt of effort, Mak angled the trunk

across his back and thrust the rooted end into a gap between the boulders. It travelled a couple of metres before becoming wedged and leaving the rest of the tree hanging at an angle.

He extended his hands like a showman. 'OK! We have a lever!' He turned to Hathi. 'You're going to have to help again. Ready?'

Mak took position at the end of the improvised lever. He used all his weight to pull on it – but only succeeded in hoisting himself off the ground.

'You're never going to move the side of a canyon,' said Diya as she urged Hathi to join Mak with a little nudge of her heels. 'Not even with an elephant. We're wasting our time.'

Mak grunted as he leaned all his weight on the lever. 'We don't need to move the entire thing. Just one . . . single . . . rock.'

At that moment, the sound of voices and scuffling feet echoed from the canyon behind them. Buldeo had caught up with them! Already!

'Hathi – help!' Mak guided the elephant's trunk to the tree and patted it. The elephant knew what was expected, strengthened his grip and heaved.

Wood creaked with the strain - yet nothing appeared to move. Then the boulder Mak had identified suddenly popped loose.

The sound of Buldeo and his henchmen grew

louder. Seconds passed and Mak's heart sank. His plan had failed.

Suddenly a loud crunch reverberated through the stack of rocks. Loose dirt trickled – then increased until it became a curtain of dust. Large rocks began to slide and then bounce down.

'Now we run!' shouted Mak.

Hathi didn't need prompting and raced ahead with Diya holding on for dear life. Mak lost his balance several times as the floor shook, but quickly recovered and sprinted after them.

The entire side of the canyon came crashing down behind them in an avalanche of debris and rock. The noise was deafening. Mak glanced over his shoulder. All he could see was a giant cloud of dust. He hoped with all his heart that the canyon was now blocked.

Then several car-sized boulders bounced out of the cloud – and headed straight for him!

CHAPTER TWENTY-EIGHT

The walls of the canyon trembled, casting more rocks and dust down from above.

One boulder bounced straight over Mak. He threw himself flat just in time to avoid being crushed, then saw another massive rock bearing down on them. He sprang to his feet and ran after Hathi and Diya.

'Move!' Mak yelled as they raced towards a bend in the canyon.

Hathi took the turn at speed, his feet skidding on loose stones making him slide into the wall. His momentum pitched Diya sideways. She threw her arms round the elephant's neck as she lost her balance and slipped right off his back. For a moment, she was running on her swollen ankle, then with a grunt of effort Diya leaped back onboard.

Mak was struggling too. The quaking ground flowed like water beneath his feet. As he took a turn, he almost slid under the elephant's feet. He caught

his balance just as another rolling boulder smashed into the curving wall behind.

Then, suddenly, they emerged from the canyon. And straight in front of them was a huge cliff.

Hathi wailed in panic, his back legs buckling as he tried to stop. His backside scraped through the earth. Diya shrieked as she slipped off his back and slid along the floor. The little elephant skidded for several metres, wailing frantically as his feet pedalled into the ground to stop him.

'*DIYA!*' Mak yelled, reaching out for her as she overtook him.

With a crunch of compacted earth, Hathi's feet dug into the ground, bringing him to an abrupt halt centimetres from plummeting over the edge.

Diya forced herself to roll, cannoning into the elephant and stopping herself. Mak stopped right on the edge too, his arms spinning to catch his balance. He bent over double to catch his breath.

'Wow, *that* was close!' he said, expelling a whoop of exhaustion and relief.

Behind them a massive plume of dust rose from the canyon mouth, obscuring everything. The rumbling continued, echoing from the valley below for almost a whole minute before fading away.

The way back was most definitely now blocked.

After coughing the dust from her mouth, Diya finally spoke up. 'Do you think . . . they survived?'

'Probably. Knowing them. They're like cockroaches,' Mak said. 'They survive everything.' He looked up at the newly formed barrier of rocks behind them. 'There's no way they'll get over that in a hurry.' Mak punched the air and gave another whoop. Not from joy but from the release of tension that had been knotting his stomach.

'Let's go!'

The path they were walking along was nothing more than a narrow ledge along the edge of the cliff, and it forced them to walk in single file. Mak led the way, with Hathi behind and Diya still on his back. She wasn't happy about sitting so high up as it made the horrible drop seem even more precarious, but she had no choice as her ankle was now even more swollen.

The good news was that the track was descending sharply and Mak was certain they'd reach the bottom within a few hours. They'd outwitted Buldeo, and Hathi would soon be reunited with his family. Mak started walking with a spring in his step.

'We should still reach Spiny Ridge tonight. Keep your eyes peeled because we should see the drone hovering over the herd, and, Hathi, you'll get to see your mum!'

'I can't believe we did this,' said Diya. 'Well, almost.'

'Nothing can stop us now!'

Mak then stopped in his tracks, his face dropping. 'Nothing . . . except *that*.'

The path ahead had reached an abrupt end, continuing far across a wide gorge. And the only thing linking them together was the flimsiest bridge they had ever seen.

CHAPTER TWENTY-NINE

'There is no way we can cross that,' Diya said flatly.

She dismounted Hathi and leaned against Mak as they stood at the edge of the bridge. A pair of steel cables had been drilled into the rock and stretched across the chasm. Wooden planks had been attached between them to form the floor.

'I told you miners came here,' said Diya. 'They must have built this.'

'That must have been a *long* time ago,' said Mak warily.

The wooden planks were heavily weathered and showed clear signs of rot. Others were missing completely. There were the remains of a hand line, which was just a hemp rope stretched at waist height across the void, but the other one had long ago rotted and fallen away.

Mak peered down. Thirty metres below lay a chasm through which a raging rapid was running.

‘At least we won’t have to worry about drowning.’ He caught Diya’s questioning look. ‘We’ll hit the rocks first,’ he pointed out.

‘Which is precisely why we can’t cross,’ Diya replied quickly.

Every fibre in Mak agreed with her, but there was one problem. ‘We can’t go back. There’s no canyon any more, remember?’

‘But there’s no way we’ll get Hathi over that!’ Diya stared at the bridge in dismay.

Mak helped her lean against a rock, then approached the first plank on the bridge. His sweaty palm gripped the handrail tightly as he placed one foot on the plank.

The bridge gave a tortured metallic twanging noise . . . but held.

Trying to hide his fear from Diya, Mak placed his other foot on the plank. Once again everything creaked but held.

He flashed a weak smile at Diya.

‘You never know until you try . . .’ Mak mumbled nervously. ‘Let me go first to see if this thing will hold . . .’

Diya raised an eyebrow. She didn’t believe it would for a second. Mak gently bounced up and down on the bridge. The wood gave a terrible creak and the cable sounded like rusty guitar strings as waves undulated across the bridge. Mak tried not to show how surprised he was that the bridge held.

'See? Completely safe.'

Diya threw up her hands in despair. 'We can't do this!'

'Diya, we don't have a choice. We either stay here and starve, or Buldeo finds a way round that landslide and decides to throw us off the edge of the canyon.'

Diya clenched her fists in frustration. She knew he was right, but that didn't change the fact that what they were about to attempt was simply insane.

Mak gave another gentle bounce on the bridge, this time with a little more confidence. 'We should go over one at a time.'

Diya gestured with an open palm. 'You first.' She paused. 'And what about Hathi?'

Mak's smile froze in place, but he found himself nodding. 'She can do it. Her balance is better than both of ours together.'

Only when he turned away did the smile melt from his face. He shuffled on to the next plank. It whined, but held. The third looked darker, perhaps completely rotten, but it was easy to step over it.

He gained confidence with each step. The bridge may be old, but it was well built. He hopped over a missing plank and, before he knew it, he was halfway

across. He turned and waved at Diya.

'See? No problem!'

He didn't want to let her see that his hand was shaking. He hurriedly continued on, the bridge swaying as he gained speed . . .

After a couple of minutes, he'd made it across without incident and waved both arms over his head.

'It's going to be OK!' he shouted back to Diya.

She took a step, but then hesitated as she peered into the gorge. She shook her head and retreated.

'I can't do it!' she shouted.

Mak wanted to yell words of encouragement, but knew it wouldn't help. From the way Diya was limping, he also realized she couldn't do it alone.

He looked at them both stood there . . . waiting. And in that moment Mak knew that if she couldn't do it alone, it was doubtful whether Hathi could either.

Fixing his resolve, Mak headed back across the bridge.

'What are you doing?' Diya asked in surprise as Mak reached her.

'Allow me.' He crooked his elbow and she slipped her arm through for support.

'Thank you, Mak,' said Diya nervously. She peeked down. 'Are you sure it's going to take the weight of us both?'

'It's going to have to, isn't it?' said Mak. 'Because next up is an elephant!'

He guided her forward. The first few metres were slow, but fine, Diya crushing his arm in terror, her other hand holding the handrail tightly . . .

Even with an injured foot, Diya made swift progress.

There's nothing like the threat of falling to your death to hurry people along, Mak thought.

They were halfway across the bridge when they heard Hathi mew nervously behind them. The little elephant had been surprisingly quiet since reaching the bridge, but, left alone, Hathi was clearly becoming anxious.

Mak stopped in the centre of the bridge and ignored Diya's little whimpers of distress as the bridge quivered. He slowly turned to Hathi.

'Don't worry, Hathi. I'll be right back.'

Mak was about to give the elephant a few more words of comfort when he saw something that made his heart sink.

Buldeo.

He was standing at the end of the narrow canyon, no more than five hundred metres behind Hathi. Mak could see they had a sturdy rope with them that they'd obviously used to climb over the landslide.

The rocks had failed to stall the thugs – and now they were closing in on the children and Hathi . . .

CHAPTER THIRTY

'RUN!' Mak yelled, shoving Diya along the bridge so hard that the whole structure swayed violently.

Diya didn't need telling twice. Even without Mak to support her, she shuffled along the bridge as fast as she could to the far side, both hands gripping the rail to support the weight of her twisted ankle.

Every worry about the lethal drop below vanished from Mak's mind as he sprinted back across the bridge towards Hathi. His only concern now was getting the elephant across before the men caught up with them.

He hopped from plank to plank with the sure-footedness he'd once felt when running high in the treetops. He reached Hathi, who was now anxiously swaying to and fro. They couldn't see Buldeo from here, but Mak was certain the elephant had picked up the thugs' scent.

Mak pushed Hathi so he was facing the bridge.

'You have to cross with me.' Mak waved his arm, but there was no telling if the elephant understood. He pulled on Hathi's trunk, leading the way, but the elephant snorted in fear and took several paces backwards.

'No!' said Mak. 'We have to do this – and now!'

He ran round behind Hathi and placed his shoulder against the elephant's backside – then he shoved. But was only rewarded with a swat across his nose from Hathi's tail, and a frightened grumble.

'Please, Hathi! You have to cross!'

Mak liked to think the elephant could understand him, that they had become friends, but then he had to remind himself that this was a wild animal who didn't understand language or the idea of friendship. He only understood actions. And, right now, the elephant could only see the drop ahead.

Mak had to think differently if he was going to win the elephant's confidence.

He moved back round and looked Hathi in the eye. He could see the intelligence behind his long lashes – but also the fear. Mak rubbed Hathi's forehead soothingly while keeping one eye over the elephant's shoulder, knowing that Buldeo was about to appear at any moment.

'You need to trust me. Follow me like you'd

follow your family. I'll be with you every step.'

Only now was it dawning on him that while the bridge *may* support the weight of an elephant, it might not support them both.

Too late to worry about that now, he thought to himself. He quickly took his shirt off.

'Makur? What are you doing?' came Diya's panicked voice from across the canyon.

There was no time to answer. He stretched his shirt over Hathi's head to cover his eyes, while still making soothing kissing noises and gently rubbing his trunk.

Like many animals, the moment the elephant couldn't see the danger, he relaxed. Mak gently tugged Hathi's trunk and was relieved when the elephant took a step forward.

'That's it! Good boy. Come on . . .'

Mak stepped on to the bridge, and the elephant followed to a cacophony of straining wood and tensing cables. The entire bridge shuddered as it took the strain. Hathi stopped as soon as he sensed the new environment.

'It's OK. It's OK . . .' Mak kept repeating the words over and over.

It worked. The elephant followed him further along the bridge. If Mak saw he was going to step on rotting wood, he'd suddenly pull Hathi forward, forcing the elephant to extend his stride to avoid the plank.

They were more than halfway across when Lalu charged round the bend and stopped dead in his tracks. His jaw hung open in astonishment when he saw the elephant crossing the narrow bridge. His breath was knocked from him when Buldeo crashed into him from behind.

'You little thief!' Buldeo yelled, pointing an accusing finger at Mak.

The sound of Buldeo's hateful voice spurred Hathi on. The elephant began to trot – and the bridge began to bounce, not with gentle motions, but with sudden harsh movements that made the cables twang ominously.

Hathi's back foot hit a rotting plank and it gave way, startling him. In a panic, Hathi tried to turn round.

'No!' Mak yanked his trunk sharply. It may have hurt, but it did the trick, stopping Hathi from walking off the edge. 'This way. Come on!' He urged the elephant onwards.

Buldeo, Lalu and Girish reached the bridge, but didn't dare set foot on it. They began to argue about who should cross in pursuit.

Mak pressed on, trying to ignore the grating noise coming from the bolts pinning the bridge into the rock next to Diya.

Diya spotted that one was working itself loose. She stamped on it, hoping her weight would be enough to secure it, and watched in horror as Girish also stepped on to the bridge.

'Hurry, Little Wolf!'

Mak didn't have to look back to know somebody else was on the bridge. The entire structure quivered alarmingly – it clearly couldn't take the extra weight. He pulled Hathi's trunk firmly.

'Run!'

Hathi responded immediately. Mak only had a few strides left before he was back on solid ground. The elephant's sudden movement had caused the planks under his feet to split – but they just about held as the pair gave one last push to reach the other side.

Just as they made it on to the rock, the bolt shot out from under Diya's foot with so much force that she was thrown backwards. With a terrible metallic *thwack*, the steel cables whipped through the air, accompanied by the crunch of splitting wood as the entire bridge was swept from under Hathi's stumbling feet. The pair had just made it on to the rock in time.

The force of the collapse ripped the one remaining hand line clean in two, and the whole structure swung wildly towards the far side where it was still anchored.

Mak couldn't tear his gaze from the bridge.

Buldeo reached out for Girish, who was clinging to the side of the bridge as it slammed into the vertical wall on the other side of the gorge.

Mak and Diya didn't hang around to see if he could hold on. They saw Lalu slip his rifle off his shoulder. Mak took his shirt from Hathi's eyes and urged the elephant to run down the curving trail and out of the men's sight just as a gunshot rang out.

CHAPTER THIRTY-ONE

The hill sloped gently downwards. It was populated with fewer trees, forced apart by massive slabs of smooth rocks that made their progress much easier. Mak, Diya and Hathi moved with a sense of renewed urgency, keen to put as much distance between them and Buldeo as possible.

They were now heading towards the sun, which was once again near the horizon, heating the rocks in its last rays.

'We're not going to make it tonight, are we?' Diya finally asked from her perch on Hathi's back.

'I don't think so,' Mak began, then corrected himself in a lower voice. 'No. I misjudged it. Tomorrow, yes, but the herd may have reached the farmers already by then. The canyon and bridge lost us a lot of time. But I . . . I totally underestimated this journey. That was a mistake.' He paused. 'I mean, if I had known how—' Just then he heard Diya laugh out loud.

'A mistake? Little Wolf. You've led us this far. Through a jungle that professional miners and loggers only managed to survive in with all of their equipment and back-up. And they weren't being chased or shot at!' She paused. 'You've been amazing.'

Praise was an unfamiliar experience for Mak. Even when he'd done something good, or earned good grades in school, all he ever got at home was the occasional pat from his mother or a causal 'you can do better' from his father. And as for his sister . . .

Diya continued. 'There is one mistake you have made, though.'

Mak's brief feel-good bubble was abruptly punctured. He caught Diya looking at him from the corner of her eye.

'You were still working on the assumption that the elephants would continue on their original course. But you didn't change it when your sister told us they were navigating *around* the hills. And even I can remember from the map—'

'It's a longer path!' they both said in unison.

Relief flooded through Mak as he watched the smile spread across Diya's face. He made a few quick mental calculations. 'The elephants would be travelling around the base of the hills, not over the top. That buys us an extra half day or more!'

Diya nodded. 'Which means we can still reach them *before* the farmers!'

Mak smiled quietly to himself and then squeezed Diya's shoulder. It was exactly the news he needed to rejuvenate his spirits.

'You're right, Diya. We can still do this. Come on, let's keep moving.'

He studied the jungle before them. Up ahead, the long sloping flat rocks disappeared into gnarly jungle where the huge trees began again and seemed thicker than ever. Once through that, he could see the path became flatter as it stretched on to Spiny Ridge.

'I say we get to the bottom of this and set up camp near the trees.'

Diya instinctively glanced behind them. 'And Buldeo?'

Mak shrugged. 'You saw that gorge. They will eventually find another point to cross. But I don't think they're going to be a problem tonight.' *Or at least I hope not*, he added silently as they pushed on.

Hathi suddenly gave a little mew and stopped. They stared at the ground ahead and froze.

Across their path, an enormous snake lay basking in the sun. It was at least twice as long as Mak. Then they suddenly became aware that there were several others scattered around, motionless on the warm rocks. A quick look behind revealed they'd walked past even more without noticing. But none were as big as the monster in front of them.

Diya patted Hathi's head reassuringly. 'Easy, Hathi.' She turned to Mak. 'It's a rock python. Even though they are not poisonous, they are incredibly powerful. They constrict their victims, crushing them to death.'

'Nice,' mumbled Mak.

While the python wasn't big enough to harm Hathi, Mak didn't fancy getting crushed to death, so they elected to walk around the big beast, respectfully leaving it to bask in the last rays. The other smaller snakes slowly started to slither off as they sensed the approaching vibrations of the trio.

Mak intentionally started to make more noise to scare off any other snakes that were in their path.

They soon reached the treeline, and Mak selected a spot next to a shorter tree filled with dark yellow star-shaped fruit that he had never seen before. He gathered as many as he could. Hathi immediately started munching and Mak quickly pushed a few aside for himself and Diya.

'I love carambolas,' Diya told him. 'They're just the best.'

Mak spent several moments crunching into the carambolas and enjoying the sweet, sticky liquid rolling down his chin.

Hathi's trunk draped over his shoulder, searching for his portion. Mak shoved it aside. 'Stop it,' he chuckled. Hathi clearly wasn't listening, and the trunk crept in as Mak bit into another fruit. Again, Mak batted it away. 'I swear you're more pig than elephant.'

Diya giggled and threw the remains of her carambola to Hathi.

'You're teaching him bad habits,' Mak warned as the trunk came over his shoulder again. He casually swept it aside with the loudest 'tut' he could manage.

Then he saw the horrified look on Diya's face. His head snapped round to see what he had really knocked off his shoulder. It was a long green snake with a triangular head that was now hissing at him from the ground. The shape of the head immediately warned him it was more than likely poisonous. But luckily it quickly slithered into the undergrowth.

'Wow!' they said in unison, and then burst out laughing.

As night began to fall, Mak suggested they sleep in the tree. There was little cover on the rocky hill, too much in the dense jungle, and he was mindful that there were many, many snakes about, attracted to the warm rocks. The trees would offer some protection, although he chose to ignore Diya's warning that snakes could easily climb trees.

He helped Diya climb up, and Hathi settled down at the base of the tree.

Night fell, and from their vantage point they could see the open sky light up in a spectacular spread of stars. The moon had waned into the shape of a toenail clipping. Dozens of shooting stars burst overhead, and the jungle played its nightly harmony of frogs and insects.

Mak felt it was like heaven. Despite the utter terror they'd experienced during the day, he couldn't think of anywhere else he'd rather be at this moment.

CHAPTER THIRTY-TWO

Mak's eyes shot open. What had woken him this time?

His vivid dreams were still fresh in his mind – dreams that Buldeo was creeping up on them. Mak strained to listen. Diya was fast asleep in the crook of a branch next to him, lying in same awkward position in which she'd fallen asleep.

Then he heard the noise he supposed had woken him. It was Hathi murmuring somewhere on the ground below them.

'Go to sleep, Hathi,' Mak said. 'You'll need all your energy for tomorrow.' The elephant wasn't listening, and now made low, hoarse yelping sounds, as if coughing. 'You'd better not be hungry,' Mak warned him as he rolled over and peered down.

It was almost too dark to make anything out. But he could just see Hathi directly under him. Then he thought he saw something he couldn't have ever imagined. There, wrapped round the terrified elephant, was the biggest rock-python Mak had ever seen.

He tried to scream at Diya, but no words came out. Just a dry scratching in his throat as he gulped for air, staring down at the snake.

If he'd thought the python basking in the sun was large, it was a baby compared to this giant. It looked almost as long as a bus and not far off a metre wide.

Hathi had tried to struggle, but the silent monster's coils had increased their grip round the elephant's chest and neck. Hathi was pushed on to his side, his sounds of distress choked from him.

'Hathi!' Mak yelled so loud that Diya bolted wide awake just in time to see Mak stand up, ready to jump.

Finally Mak had found his voice: 'Hathi's in trouble! Big trouble, Diya!'

And, with that, Mak dived from the tree. He was acting on instinct, not logic, hoping, praying, that the bulk of the snake would break his fall.

Mak landed hard on the reptile, causing its great head to snap round to face him. A tongue the size of Mak's forearm shot out as the beast sensed the new threat.

He felt the powerful muscles ripple and swell beneath the smooth skin. Reaching into his pocket,

Mak quickly pulled out his penknife. He glanced down as he fumbled to open the blade in the dark – and when he looked up, the snake was facing him with jaws opened.

Mak froze as he peered inside the snake's mouth. It was the size of a sewage pipe, and smelt just as bad. Its grip on Hathi loosened just a little – and its body slithered under Mak as the head coiled back, preparing to attack him.

Mak leaped off the snake, hit the ground and rolled to his feet in one smooth motion. But he found himself standing with his back in the folds of a huge tree root with nowhere to move. The snake lunged for Mak, and the world seemed to move in slow motion. Mak watched as the snake's jaws dislodged and hyper-extended to a size that could easily swallow a football.

Mak tensed with his penknife outstretched, hoping the blade could somehow defend him.

Then, with a meaty thud, something careened into the side of the snake's head – knocking it off target. The python's blunt nose slammed into the tree roots a centimetre from Mak, but with such force that the bark split.

Just as suddenly, Mak's world resumed normal speed.

Diya had saved him, leaping down from the tree

and brandishing a thick branch she'd broken off. She'd struck the snake with such force that Mak could see the blood seeping from under its scales. Diya bounced off the snake's head, and crashed into a bush – screaming in pain as she landed on her twisted ankle.

Mak sprinted to help her stand. The snake's tail was still round Hathi, but had slackened enough to allow the elephant to breathe.

The python swivelled round to face the humans, its tongue flicking, as if in a last burst of anger and effort. It reared up, already taller than Mak.

Diya's tales of loggers eaten alive came flooding back to him. No longer fairy tales, but hard facts. Monster-sized snakes really did exist in the jungle. And this one was ready to kill them both.

CHAPTER THIRTY-THREE

Being so close to the giant python, Mak could see its muscles tense. He pushed Diya behind him, hoping she'd have the sense to run if the snake bit him.

'Get away!' Mak bellowed.

The snake's jaws extended once more as it prepared to strike.

Mak needed to think fast.

He crouched down and scooped up a whole armful of dead leaves from the ground, and like a confetti firework he launched the bundle of leaves and earth right at the snake's hissing head.

The python, confused, struck blindly at the leaves, and in the briefest of moments Mak had darted away from the snake, avoiding its head.

Like a gazelle, he ran round the snake and started tugging on the heavy coils still looped round Hathi. He pulled with all his might, but the python was still holding the squirming elephant fast.

Hathi kicked out, trying to free a leg, as Mak kept uncoiling the snake's body. Its hissing head swung round to deal with the annoyance, once and for all. Mak stumbled back again just as Hathi was now beginning to wrestle free from the snake's grasp. But in the darkness, there was no way to see that behind Mak was a steep slope – and Mak tripped, finding himself tumbling down the embankment.

Rocks and branches thumped his back and chest as he rolled head over heels. Then his head bumped against a rock, and the metallic taste of blood dripped into his mouth as he came to rest several metres away.

Mak tried to sit upright, but the world around him spun and he could still see lights dancing across his vision . . .

Lights?

No . . . they were *real* lights. Bright torches bobbing at the top of the embankment – and with them clear loud voices shouting in Hindi. It was Buldeo and his men!

Mak tried to crawl back up the slope. A wave of dizziness struck him and he staggered sideways into the earth. He could just make out Buldeo and Girish slashing the snake with machetes. The serpent relinquished its grip on Hathi and turned on the new threat with a loud hiss.

A gunshot rang out and the snake jolted for a second. Lalu stood to the side with his rifle, and quickly began to focus for another shot. He barely had time to position his rifle against his shoulder to fire before the snake lashed out at him, and bit him square on the shoulder, sinking its teeth into flesh and bone.

Lalu let out a blood-curdling scream, but almost instantly the snake swung the rest of its body over and began to wrap its deadly coils round him.

Lalu's screaming pierced the night. Buldeo

lunged at the reptile, blindly hitting out with a rock he'd picked up, striking its head where it was attached to Lalu's shoulder. The beast recoiled, hissing.

It had released Lalu, but now lunged out wildly at its new attacker.

Mak just made out Buldeo rolling aside and Lalu fleeing into the darkness with another terrified scream.

He tried to stand again, but his swimming head made him sway and he fell backwards, sliding further down the slope. He reached out to grab anything to help him stand, but his vision was blurring, and he collapsed to the ground once more.

In the criss-crossing torch beams dancing at the top of the slope, he watched Buldeo and Girish continuing to slash at the snake with repeated blows from their machetes. It was gruesome, but finally the snake gave up the fight and lay there dead, although its muscles kept twitching violently, looking as if it might come alive again at any moment.

Mak couldn't help but feel a twinge of sympathy for the python that had only been trying to hunt for a meal – even a human one.

He fought a sense of grogginess. From where he lay, he saw Hathi stand, freed from the snake's coils. But the fight had weakened the elephant and he was in no condition to fend off Buldeo as a thick rope was thrown round his neck.

Mak heard Diya scream as the men found her, and Hathi whimpered in fear . . .

Then, for Mak, everything went dark.

CHAPTER THIRTY-FOUR

It was still dark when Mak woke.

His head was thumping. A quick check with his hand revealed that the blow to the side of his skull was small, and the blood had dried, even if it was still tender. He scrambled to the top of the embankment in the darkness.

Everybody had gone, Hathi included. The enormous snake lay dead among the ferns. Mak ran his hand along its still-warm flank and felt a pang of pity. He'd hoped he could free Hathi and let the snake live; it had survived so many years in the untouched forest only to be butchered the moment it had encountered man.

Mak searched the area methodically on his hands and knees. It was too dark to make out any details, but he was desperate to find Hathi's tracks. His careful sweeping of the ground was rewarded when he found his penknife. He pocketed it and continued searching, forcing himself to cover small square areas so he didn't overlook anything or double-back on himself.

The technique worked.

He stumbled across Lalu's belt, poking from the grass, still with his torch and machete hanging from it. The last he'd seen of Lalu was the man running for his life into the jungle. Had he not returned? Had he got lost? Or run off the cliff, maybe? There was no way of knowing.

Steeling himself, Mak unclipped the blade and torch. At first the torch wouldn't switch on, but a quick thump brought it to life. With the batteries nearly drained, the beam wasn't strong, but it was enough for him to spot Hathi's tracks leading into the jungle, complete with those of Buldeo and Girish.

He hoped that Diya had been loaded on to Hathi's back.

Mak felt for the pouch on his trousers and was relieved to find the satellite phone still inside. He weighed the phone in his hand, debating whether he should call his sister for help, now the situation was so serious. Diya had been kidnapped by a pair of cutthroats who hadn't hesitated to shoot at them, and he had no way of knowing if she was still alive.

But what could his sister do to help? A search

party wouldn't be able to reach them any time soon, and he didn't even know exactly where they were, anyway. Helicopters had nowhere to land, and if anybody did locate them, Buldeo and Girish would have already vanished into the jungle.

Mak put the satellite phone away, thinking hard. He was on his own. It was up to him to find his friends before it was too late.

The torch was necessary for Mak to navigate through the thick jungle. In places, the darkness was so intense it seemed to swallow the dim beam of light. Under the thick canopy there was no breeze, and the air smelt stagnant and felt overly warm.

The dense foliage left regular signs of the group's passing. Branches had been snapped by Hathi, the ground churned by their collective heavy footsteps. Buldeo was obviously not worried about anybody following them. He supposed that the men were keen not to run into any more colossal snakes in this part of uncharted wilderness.

Eventually, when he started to feel dizzy, Mak was forced to stop and rest for several minutes. He had no idea how long he'd been unconscious, but was surprised at how far Buldeo had managed to travel.

He switched off his torch to save the battery

and made himself close his eyes. When he opened them after several minutes, he saw an array of subtle blue and green lights speckled across the trees like miniature star fields. It was the jungle's bioluminescence – chemicals within insects and plants giving off the faintest light. It was a rare and beautiful sight to behold.

Glow bugs zipped around his head with carefree abandon. Mak felt himself relax for an unguarded moment, almost letting himself fall asleep . . .

He jolted himself awake just in time. 'Do NOT nod off!' he said aloud. He shook his head to fend off sleep. He couldn't afford to stop and nap – that would only increase Buldeo's lead. He rubbed the cut on the side of his head and wondered if the blow was clouding his senses.

Onwards. That was the only option he had. Sleep could wait.

He estimated that he'd walked for another thirty minutes before the trees thinned out. Occasional patches of star-spangled sky could be seen overhead, and a gentle breeze now blew away the cloying stuffy atmosphere.

Up ahead was a light. Mak had to rub his eyes to make sure fatigue wasn't playing tricks with his mind. No. He saw what he saw. It was a campfire.

Cautiously, he crept a little closer. Then he lay still and waited, his heart thumping. All remained quiet. He plucked up all the courage he could muster and crept even closer.

Soon he could make out things in their camp. He could clearly see Hathi, roped to a tree. Next to the elephant was Diya crouched on the ground, her hands bound together. And flanking her on each side were Buldeo and Girish.

Lalu was nowhere to be seen.

But, still, how on earth was Mak ever going to overpower the remaining two men, both armed with rifles, and save his friends?

CHAPTER THIRTY-FIVE

Diya struggled against her bonds with renewed energy, but still the ropes held. She glanced at Buldeo and Girish, who now lay by the fire.

Girish snored and rolled to his other side; Buldeo rubbed his eyes as he fought to stay awake on lookout duty.

The men's clothes were stained with the snake's blood, which they'd tried to clean off using water from a small brook that gurgled through the glade they'd chosen for camp. Their outer clothes hung from sticks close to the fire, and damp boots were hung upside down to dry.

Hathi was tied to a tree next to Diya. The rope round his neck had turned his skin red raw where he had attempted to break it, and now his rebellious spirit appeared crushed. He stood silent, head down. Beaten.

During the rush through the jungle, Buldeo

had threatened Diya's life if she should scream or struggle. She knew what a vile man he was, and was terrified that if she didn't escape soon, then Buldeo would run out of reasons to keep her alive.

Just then she heard a noise.

'Pssst!'

Diya flinched, expecting a snake to rise from the bushes. She looked around when she heard it again . . . then she craned her head upwards—

Little Wolf! she almost shouted, but quickly checked herself.

Mak was suspended upside down from the branches above her. He put a finger to his lips, winked and disappeared back into the tree. Diya had no idea what he had planned, but one thing she had learned was to trust this boy.

Mak had circled the entire campsite in case Buldeo had laid any snares or tripwires, but had found nothing. If the men thought Mak was still alive, they didn't seem too concerned about him turning up.

That was their first mistake.

On his target recce, he had been forced to work with the light from the campfire. And it had almost proved disastrous.

He'd blundered into a thorny bush that cut his arm, belly-crawled through a stream that had soaked him to the bone, and almost walked headlong into a rotting stump that was the home of several nasty-looking scorpions with tails that quivered threateningly. They may have been small, but the oversized venom glands on their tails told him that the poison in them would do very nasty things.

Only once did he think Buldeo had heard him, and that was when he reached Hathi. The elephant snorted in what Mak knew was delight. Mak pressed flat against the tree as Buldeo looked round and told the elephant to shut up.

The last thing Mak needed was for Buldeo to become curious or to come over and check on the elephant.

He'd decided to climb the tree and work his way to a position above Diya so he could lower himself right next to her. He hoped that up above was the last place Buldeo would think of keeping watch.

Diya's determined smile was enough to convince him that she was fit enough for their escape, but even in the low light he noticed that the boot on her injured foot was unlaced wide open, and her swollen ankle looked more like a ball.

Escaping quickly on foot would be impossible.

He needed to neutralize the threat. But the men were too big to face in a fight.

Armed only with a penknife, satellite phone and a

torch, Mak pondered on what he could do.

His choices were limited.

As he slipped back down from the tree, he shook that thought from his head. No, he had survived for weeks in the jungle on his own. He knew that limited options just meant a lack of imagination. He needed to think like a survivor once more.

Mak looked around the jungle and then smiled.

Of course – he was surrounded by options . . .

CHAPTER THIRTY-SIX

Buldeo checked Girish was still asleep before pulling out the small metal flask hidden in his jerkin. He took a swig of the whiskey inside. The sharp taste was enough to rekindle his senses once more.

Buldeo and Girish had considered using the elephant to haul the giant snake's carcass out of the jungle. Something that big might be worth a fortune to a collector, but they'd decided instead to leave it and focus on getting the elephant back to civilization. Back to work. That was their priority now.

Stifling a yawn, Buldeo looked over to check on his prisoners. They were still there and hadn't moved. He calculated that by late afternoon tomorrow, they would reach the area used by loggers and would be able to hitch a lift back to town. Between now and then he had to figure out what to do with the girl. Perhaps it would be best to leave her tied to the tree? The jungle would take care of her eventually . . .

He closed his eyes and used his backpack as a pillow, his toes warming near the fire. He wouldn't sleep, he assured himself, just allow his eyes to rest as the warmth from the whiskey flowed through his veins.

Mak had been waiting patiently for an opportunity. Just when he considered asking Diya to create a distraction, he saw Buldeo's eyes close.

Mak didn't waste any time. He slipped off his shirt and wrapped it round one hand. He was going to need protection for his plan. Crawling on all fours, ignoring the sharp twigs and stones scratching his bare tummy, he headed straight for the rotting tree stump.

A quick prod inside exposed several angry-looking scorpions. Using his protected hand, he quickly plucked them up by the tail and dropped them into the rest of the shirt, which he splayed open like a sheet.

With four angry scorpions waving their tails, Mak gathered the corners of his shirt into a pouch and, as stealthily as he could, crawled over to where the clothes were drying near the fire.

Mak took care to make sure the men's hanging

jackets were between him and Buldeo, acting as a screen.

He reached the boots and gingerly took them off the branches from where they hung. Placing them on the ground, he carefully slipped a scorpion into each boot. He waited a minute to check they weren't crawling out, knowing that they'd like a dark, damp place in which to hide.

So far, so good. Then he hung the boots back on the branches.

Suddenly Buldeo jerked awake.

Mak caught sight of him from round the edge of the shirt. The man was looking straight at him . . .

Mak felt a shiver run though him. He expected Buldeo to shout and scream, but instead the man just stared. Then he took a stick and poked the fire, pushing another log into the flames. Staring at the bright flames had all but ruined Buldeo's night vision, and Mak realized he was concealed just enough to remain invisible if he didn't move.

He forced himself to stay still and wait for Buldeo to lie back and close his eyes.

A few tense minutes later, Mak crawled backwards to the safety of darkness. He circled the camp and emerged behind Diya, placing his hand over her mouth so she didn't say anything. His penknife easily severed her bonds and he helped her stand. She gave a sharp intake of breath the moment she put any weight on her ankle.

'You're going to have to ride Hathi again,' Mak whispered.

They moved to the elephant, making low shushing noises in the hope that he didn't bellow loudly with excitement. Hathi seemed to understand the need for silence, and the moment Mak cut the rope from his neck he trotted into the deeper jungle with barely a sound.

Hathi's trunk brushed across Mak's face in thanks. Mak scratched him between the eyes, then helped Diya on to the elephant's back.

'Come on,' he whispered. 'We don't have much time.'

They had less time than he thought. He suddenly heard a shout of alarm from the camp as Buldeo woke up and found his captive missing.

'Go!' hissed Mak, shoving Hathi in the direction he'd identified would take them back towards their destination.

Mak ran ahead with the torch in one hand, leading a way for them through the undergrowth. Hathi kept close behind as the men's voices rose in anger. Mak couldn't resist a quick look behind.

During all the shouting, he knew that Buldeo and Girish would be snatching at their boots to get ready to give chase.

It was with a deep sense of glee that Mak heard a piercing scream as one of the men thrust his foot into his boot.

Buldeo had toppled backwards, into Girish, who was also howling in pain. Both men rolled into the fire, casting embers everywhere.

The last thing Mak saw was the men rolling in the stream to put out the flames that singed their clothes, while at the same time clawing at their boots with increasingly deranged screams.

Then the men were lost in the darkness, their hollering fading away. And Mak felt a surge of pride that he had just saved his friends . . .

CHAPTER THIRTY-SEVEN

There was only so far they could run in the dead of night. Mak decided they should stop when they reached a wide but shallow river. His torch was beginning to die and he knew that the risk of getting hopelessly lost almost outweighed Buldeo and Girish catching up with them.

Hathi stood in the water drinking deeply as Diya and Mak sat on a large boulder and stared at the stars overhead.

'Thank you for saving me. Us, I mean,' said Diya.

'Never leave a man behind.' Mak grinned. 'Or a girl or an elephant. Especially not a friend.'

They both closed their eyes, chatting about anything but the horrors of the giant snake and their capture . . . and before they knew it, they were fast asleep.

Mak woke with a start, annoyed that he'd fallen asleep. The faint dawn light made the landscape appear dusty. He was relieved to see there was no sign of anybody else. Hathi was reaching as high as he could to pull tender leaves from a tree, while Diya was already awake and soaking her ankle in the cold running water.

'Morning,' she said, lifting her foot for inspection. The cold had helped the swelling go down, but it was still badly bruised.

'You should have woken me,' said Mak, stretching. He slid down from the boulder to join her.

'Why? I think you did enough last night to earn a little sleep. Besides, I kept busy by making myself a crutch.' She picked up a Y-shaped branch, which she had shaped with the machete to be the right size. 'And breakfast.'

Mak's face broke into a grin as she held up a pair of fish, using her fingers to hook them under the gills. 'How did you do that?'

'I was born and raised here,' she reminded him. 'You don't grow up in the jungle without learning a thing or two.'

Mak made a small fire, lighting it with his last waterproof match, while Diya used the penknife to delicately cut the fish open and gut it. Mak remembered when that kind of action would have made him feel squeamish, but since he'd been forced to eat raw meat in the wild, that revulsion had disappeared. Instead, he watched hungrily, appreciating her skill.

They were picking the last morsels of flesh from the fish spines when Mak decided he had put off the inevitable for long enough. He took the satellite phone out and they both stared at it. The broad banks of the river gave them a good enough view of Spiny Ridge. They could see the nape of the valley where, from the air at least, it tapered into a V. The very place they hoped to intercept Hathi's herd.

'You have to call her,' said Diya gently. She indicated above them. 'And you will get the best reception here.'

It had been two days since he'd convinced his sister they were birdwatching close to base camp. It would certainly have been noticed that he and Diya were missing by now. He'd faced wolves, leopards, killer monkeys, poachers, madmen and giant snakes in this jungle, but his hands were trembling at the thought of speaking to his sister or his parents. He thumbed the power on. The screen illuminated, showing only one bar of battery remaining. His throat went dry as he dialled Anula's number.

She answered it almost immediately. 'Mak?'

'Hey, sis—'

'Where the heck are you?' She sounded panicky.

'With Diya—'

'I know you're with her. Everybody is going crazy. I covered for you for the first day and night, but since then Mum and Dad and everyone else here have been sick with worry. I had to tell them.' She paused to catch her breath. 'We were beginning to fear the worst. I mean, we hadn't heard anything from you. Where exactly are you?'

Mak hesitated. He'd never meant to put his sister in such a difficult position. He felt guilty.

'I'm sorry, sis. I love you. We're OK.' He paused. 'We're in the jungle. I mean . . . quite a long way in.' He heard the harsh intake of breath on the end of the line. He talked faster so she couldn't get a word in edgeways. 'I don't have much battery life left on this phone and we desperately need your help. We rescued an elephant, a baby, from the village and are bringing him back to the herd. The same herd Anil is monitoring. We're very close to them now, but I need you to get on the drone and find out exactly where they are.'

The silence on the line forced him to check the phone hadn't died. Then Anula spoke again. She sounded out of breath.

'I heard about that in the village. Everybody

thought it had escaped on its own.'

'Anula, I need that drone—'

There was silence except for the muffled sound of running footsteps.

The battery icon was now blinking in warning.

Then he heard the clack of a keyboard as Anula accessed the drone.

'Right, I see them. They haven't deviated from the path they were on and . . . I can see your satellite phone signal. You're just over the hill. If you head slightly north-west . . .'

For Diya's purposes, Mak pointed in the direction. 'We'll get ahead of them?'

'Yes. Hold on. Anil had the drone positioned a little way off . . . the cameras have longer range. I can see the village they're heading towards.' She paused. 'Mak. It's bad.'

'What?'

'It looks like they've dug trenches and are setting up some very nasty logs. Sharpened to points. Mak, I think they're—'

That was the moment the phone's battery decided to die.

CHAPTER THIRTY-EIGHT

Mak and Diya travelled fast but in silence, lost in their own thoughts at what lay ahead.

Mak regularly checked their course against the sun, aware that even the slightest detour could cause a delay that would bring the herd into conflict with the farmers.

Diya rode on Hathi's back. The elephant was now used to his passenger and had even quickened his pace. Mak was certain the little elephant knew his family was close at hand. He'd read reports that elephants could sense ultra-low frequency waves through their feet and they could communicate that way. He wondered just how true that was.

By noon their stomachs were rumbling, but still they didn't stop for food. 'We won't starve to death,' said Mak as they passed trees laden with fruit. 'We have to keep moving.'

They finally crested Spiny Ridge and stopped

to check their direction. From midway down the ridge, the trees had been cleared and the ground transformed into a patchwork of fields. At the very bottom of the hill was a small village of basic thatched huts. Mak counted thirty-four. They could even smell the wood fires as smoke drifted from huts, making the air hazy.

A wide dirt track cut through the village, and beyond that the jungle started again.

Then they spotted what Anula had also seen from the drone.

A barrier of logs had been thrust into the soil at forty-five degree angles, their sharpened points ready to skewer anything emerging from the jungle. Trenches had been dug and, as they watched, a farmer ignited them. A terrifying wall of flames shot a dozen feet in the air.

'Little Wolf. Look up! Over there!'

Mak had to shield his eyes from the sun to see Diya was pointing at a smudge in the sky.

'A bird?' he guessed.

'No. It's not moving. It's the drone. We've got to go!'

As they hurried down the side of the hill, Mak could see that the whole village was watching them. Men, women and children stared at them with a mixture of curiosity and suspicion. Several farmers had guns over their shoulders. They were old rifles, but that didn't dull their danger.

'They are nervous, and that makes them dangerous,' Diya muttered under her breath.

'I can understand that,' Mak said quietly. 'They are all ready to defend their village against a herd of elephants, and we come along instead.'

Mak also knew they looked battered and dishevelled, but he drew himself to his full height and raised his hands as if in surrender, while trying to muster the warmest smile he could.

'Please can we speak to whoever is in charge,' Mak said slowly, his hands in a prayer position in front of him.

Nobody replied and the air of suspicion became thicker.

'We are here to help.' He looked pleadingly at Diya who repeated his words in Hindi. That got a reaction from the crowd.

An old man, his back hunched from years of hard labour, stepped forward. He used a staff to support his frail frame.

'I am in charge,' he said in English, with a stronger voice than Mak expected.

Mak nodded his head respectfully. 'Sir, we have travelled far to be here through many dangers. This calf belongs to the approaching herd. They don't mean you any harm. They don't want your crops – they just want their baby, and your village is right in their path.'

Again, the elder translated, and Mak sensed the mood around him darken. Diya gasped as rifles were pulled off shoulders and their bolts *click-clacked*. Mak stepped in front of Hathi and raised his hands.

'No! Stop! This is not the way!'

The elder looked grimly at Mak.

'The elephants come only to destroy.'

'But not if they find what they are looking for,' Mak interjected, pointing at Hathi.

The elder paused. Then continued to speak. 'We will protect our village at any cost. That is all I have to say.'

CHAPTER THIRTY-NINE

The elder was about to continue rebuking Mak, but stopped when loud chattering suddenly broke out. They were all looking towards their fortifications and pointing.

The drone had finally drifted into view, high in the sky. One villager raised his rifle to take a shot.

'NO!' Mak yelled as he ran over and put his hands up to stop the man from shooting. Despite being several feet taller – and wider – than Mak, the man stopped in surprise.

'You have to trust us!' Mak panted.

With a gentle nudge of her heels, Diya urged Hathi forward. The crowd hastily parted for the calf, and then Diya started to speak in rapid Hindi, her voice carrying powerfully as she gestured at Mak.

Mak had no idea what she was saying, but saw the villagers were now looking at him curiously. The elder's eyes narrowed as he listened carefully.

When Diya finished, the crowd began to talk to the elder.

'What did you say?' Mak asked out of the corner of his mouth.

'I told them about you surviving in the jungle. They've heard the stories about you, even out here. I told them about rescuing Hathi from those thugs and how you fought the snake and saved us from bandits.'

'I didn't really fight the snake,' he whispered back.

Diya didn't look at him, but her voice lowered. 'You got in a few good punches . . . and I was a little fuzzy on the details.'

The village elder silenced the crowd with a single barked command. Then he turned to Mak.

'We do not wish to kill the elephants, only to defend our lands.' He paused as if the next words were difficult to say. 'What do you suggest we do, Little Wolf?'

'Oh, and I told them your spirit name,' Diya added sheepishly.

Mak pointed towards the drone. 'That is a camera drone tracking the elephants. Any minute now they are going to walk out of the forest. All they want is their son.' He gestured to Hathi. 'Then they'll turn aound and leave you alone. You need to give us a chance. You need to give *them* a chance.'

The elder weighed up Mak's words, then finally gave a single nod of consent.

Diya dismounted Hathi and hobbled on her crutch as Mak led the elephant towards the wall of trees. The village elder had instructed his people to extinguish the flames in the trenches so the herd wouldn't be frightened away, but he refused to lower the sharp log barrier.

Mak and Diya waited nervously. Mak scratched Hathi's forehead as the little elephant peered into the dark jungle, ears gently flapping as he searched for any sound.

'I'm going to miss you, buddy,' Mak said. He felt a lump in his throat, and when he looked at Diya he was relieved to see that she also had tears in her eyes as she gently whispered to the elephant in Hindi.

He wiped his eyes discreetly.

The drone silently drifted into view overhead and Mak wondered if his family was now watching. He hoped so.

Hathi then suddenly reacted, drawing Mak's attention back to the trees – and his heart leaped into his mouth. A dozen fully grown elephants stood before him, appearing as silent as statues.

Up close they were huge. The leader was twice Mak's height.

She gently snorted and Hathi came running to her side. Their trunks coiled as they were reunited, and the little elephant mewed with delight.

The elephants regarded Mak and Diya warily. The children knew that being this close to a wild elephant was incredibly dangerous. But somehow it also felt so safe.

Just then, with the faintest of sounds, the elephants quietly turned their backs on the village

and melted away, back into the jungle.

Mak raised his hand and waved. 'Bye, Hathi.'

He had hoped the little elephant would stop and wave its trunk in farewell. That's what happened in movies – but Hathi didn't look back.

'Maybe animals don't understand goodbye,' said Mak, his voice cracking with emotion.

Diya hooked his arm and leaned against him. 'No. But they understand family.'

Even as Hathi disappeared into the jungle, they could still hear his trumpets of delight . . . and, Mak hoped, maybe even one of farewell.

They both wiped away their tears as they returned to the farmers, who had been watching from a safe distance. The elder smiled with admiration.

'That was quite something, Little Wolf.'

Mak suddenly felt drained as the effort from the last few days began to catch up with him.

The elder extended his arm towards a hut. 'Please, eat with us. Rest. We have a truck and can take you to the logging town before nightfall.'

'Home,' Diya said quietly.

Mak let her lean on him as they followed the elder to his hut; their stomachs were already grumbling.

'Do you think our families are going to be mad with us?' she asked.

'Probably,' Mak replied. 'But I just hope they will

have seen what happened on the drone.' He paused. 'I still think we did the right thing.' He reached for her hand. 'And I would do it all again. For Hathi, of course.'

Diya smiled. 'Of course.'

THE END

TURN THE PAGE FOR MORE TIPS ON HOW TO SURVIVE IN THE JUNGLE

NAVIGATION

It's important to keep a map and compass with you and know how to navigate with them when surviving in the outdoors. But after Mak and Diya lose their map in the jungle, they're forced to navigate by the position of the sun and the landmarks around them.

- To navigate using the watch method, lay your watch flat with the hour hand pointing towards the sun and make sure your eye is at the same level as the watch.

- Draw an imaginary line between the twelve o'clock position and the hour hand – that direction is south (in the northern hemisphere).

- From there, figure out which direction you need to go in and take a note of any prominent landmarks along the way (hills/unusual trees/changes in the landscape) and what your destination should look like.

- Stop periodically to check your position using the watch method.

FIRE

Diya teaches Mak a few new tricks in *Return to the Jungle* – one of them is how to make a covert fire, or snake-hole fire, great for when you don't want the smoke to give you away.

- Dig two holes a few paces apart, one much smaller than the other. Then drive a stick through the earth to create a small tunnel, or chimney between the two.

- Build the fire in the larger hole, beginning with kindling such as dry moss and twigs, and gradually building up a tepee shape with larger sticks and logs.

- Once you light the fire, the smoke and oxygen will be pulled through the makeshift chimney into the smaller chamber, keeping smoke to a minimum and making sure the heat stays in.

- Make sure to put the fire out thoroughly before leaving your camp.

TRACKING

Mak and Diya meet plenty of animals during their travels through the jungle, some of them very dangerous, and it helps to be able to know what to look out for.

Keeping your wits about you is very important and a great way to practise is by playing Kim's Game, inspired by a game described in Rudyard Kipling's novel *Kim.* Gather a number of items from around the house and place them on a tray. Then try to memorize as much as you can about them. Putting the tray out of sight, describe their features and position in relation to the other items on the tray as accurately as you can. It is a technique used by survival experts all over the world.

- Once you know how to memorize things, you need to learn what you're looking for, and identifying animal footprints is a great way to start. The quality of animal tracks can vary a lot depending on the ground they are on – fresh prints tend to show up darker than old prints, or if there is rain on the surface of the footprint, the animal will have passed by before the rain.

- Different animals have different patterns of walking – for example, footprints in a diagonal formation can be from four-legged animals which move two legs at the same time (dogs, cats and animals with hoofs, like the gaurs Mak and Diya meet).

- You can also follow the direction an animal has travelled without footprints to guide you, by looking for signs of disturbance in the landscape around you. Bent grass, trampled or darker patches of vegetation, hair or fur caught on branches, and even animal droppings can give you a sense of how recently and in what direction they passed you!

ABOUT THE AUTHOR

Bear Grylls has become known around the world as one of the most recognized faces of survival and outdoor adventure. Trained from an early age in martial arts, and taught to climb and sail by his father, Bear went on to spend three years as a soldier in the British Special Forces, serving with 21 SAS, before becoming one of the youngest-ever climbers of Mount Everest.

Since then he has gone on to host more extreme-adventure TV shows across more global networks than anyone else in the world, including the BAFTA award-winning *The Island with Bear Grylls*, *Bear Grylls' Survival School*, *Man vs. Wild*, *Running Wild* for NBC and *Absolute Wild* for Chinese TV. He is an honorary Colonel to the Royal Marine Commandos and the youngest-ever Chief Scout, an inspiration to forty million Scouts worldwide.

He is also a family man, and a number-one bestselling author, with dozens of books to his name, including his autobiography, *Mud, Sweat and Tears*. *Return to the Jungle* is Bear's second book in the New Jungle Book Adventures series with Macmillan Children's Books, the sequel to *Spirit of the Jungle*.

COULD YOU SURVIVE IN THE JUNGLE?

After being washed away down the Wainganga River during a flash flood, Mak wakes up alone in the Indian jungle.

The jungle is full of danger – poisonous snakes, cunning monkeys and desperate poachers – and every step Mak takes might be his last.

Mak finds help and friendship from other jungle creatures, but he will need all his skill and luck to survive and make his way back home.

A heart-stopping contemporary adventure inspired by Rudyard Kipling's classic* The Jungle Book*, from real-life adventurer Bear Grylls